NO NAME ON MY GRAVE

SAM RAVEN
BOOK SIX

BRIAN DRAKE

ROUGH
EDGES
PRESS

No Name on my Grave
Paperback Edition
Copyright © 2025 (As Revised) Brian Drake

Rough Edges Press
An Imprint of Wolfpack Publishing
1707 E. Diana Street
Tampa, FL 33610

roughedgespress.com

Paperback ISBN 978-1-68549-454-4
Ebook ISBN 978-1-68549-453-7

I dedicated a recent Sam Raven book to our cat Buster, who has always left his marks on my manuscripts, usually by walking on the pages after going through the mud outside. This book is dedicated to his memory. We lost him as 2022 began.

NO NAME ON MY GRAVE

PROLOGUE

THE THREE TWO-AND-A-HALF TON TRUCKS, LOADED WITH armed men and munitions, rumbled at a moderate pace along the rutted jungle road. The engines chugged, sending pungent exhaust fumes into the sky. Sam Raven was already wet from the humidity; he didn't need the smell.

He said to the woman beside him, "Wait!"

But Lucy Pinto didn't listen. The camo-clad woman leaned over the edge of the roadside ditch, pushing through covering foliage to snap rapid pictures with her digital camera.

Raven grimaced and clicked off the safety of his Kalashnikov AK-103. If any of the gunners on the trucks noticed Lucy, they'd shoot. He and Lucy would have to fight and run and probably get killed; so much for the mission. But the last truck drove by their position, and nobody saw them—still, it was a close call they didn't need. Raven told her so.

"My people need to know what we face," she said. She tapped the camera screen to send the pictures to the main fighting force a few miles behind them.

"We've known what we face for a week now," Raven said.

"These reinforcements only confirm we're running out of time."

She returned the camera to her BDU blouse. The fatigues were almost too big for her petite size. She'd cut extra holes in her belt to tighten it properly. "You're unhappy with me?"

"You know better."

"It's not your brother who's a hostage, Raven."

"And you being reckless will only get you killed. Then what?"

She stared at him. Raven scoffed and turned away. He watched the road for more activity.

Some fighters, despite their experience, still made stupid mistakes. But Lucy was right. His brother wasn't held prisoner at a narco-terrorist camp in the middle of El Salvador. His interest wasn't personal, but instead *surgical*.

The trucks were on their way to a camp of narco-terrorists lead by a man named Xavier Fuentes. Raven had been in pursuit of Fuentes for two weeks. The killer had met with contacts in Spain and Portugal, but slipped away before Raven delivered a kill shot. Two frustrating weeks of near misses and lost opportunities.

Fuentes and his unit of freelance killers worked for any cartel willing to pay their fee. In exchange, they set off bombs in populated areas, targeted police and politicians—whatever it took to shed the blood of those opposed to the drug business.

For Raven, it was another challenge in his war without end, and he was a man made for war. He'd once donned the uniform of the 82nd Airborne and 5th Special Forces Group. Later, he'd traded his officer patch for the anonymity of the CIA's Ground Branch. Now he worked on his own. No uniform. No home base. Just vengeance for those without a champion.

Raven intended to forever close down Fuentes and his

reign of violence. But he had help he hadn't counted on to make up for the resources he lacked.

—————————

AFTER HIS ARRIVAL in El Salvador seven days earlier, Raven tracked Fuentes to a hotel and booked a room on the same floor as the narco killer.

He followed Fuentes and his two-man entourage as they enjoyed a night out. At a popular nightclub, Raven made notes of every person Fuentes held court with—a rotating gallery of rogues. Fuentes was entertaining offers.

He thought meeting Lucy Pinto in the midst of the crowded club meant he had screwed up. The enemy had seen him and sent a honeytrap to get him out of the way. But Raven knew a few tricks. He wanted to reverse the trap and learn a thing or two from the fiery dark-eyed beauty they'd sicced onto him.

He brought her back to his hotel room for an energetic romp on the king-sized bed. Afterwards, when they lay still catching their breath, she'd jammed the muzzle of a Colt .38 revolver into his belly. He never asked her where she'd kept it while nude.

"Target practice in bed," he told her instead, "isn't a kink I'm into."

"You're lucky I don't shoot your balls off, *murderer*," and she cocked the gun. Raven moved fast. He covered the revolver with one hand, jamming the web of his right hand between the hammer and frame, and grabbed her neck with the other. He rolled on top of Lucy to pin her to the mattress.

They sorted out the misunderstanding quickly. Lucy and "her people" thought Raven was with Fuentes, visiting El Salvador to join the narco-killer on a hit. He thought she was on Fuentes's payroll with orders to kill him. Once he explained his reason for being there, and she told him *her* reason, they both calmed down. She put the .38 away and they talked some more.

Lucy Pinto represented a vigilante unit out of Colombia called *El Tigre*. They were a group of strike-and-hide commandos who'd declared war on the cartels in response to ineffective government efforts to curb the drug trade. Every member of *El Tigre* had lost a loved one to drug violence, and Lucy was no exception—a bomb planted by Fuentes killed her parents, making her and her brother orphans.

Raven met with the squad sent to El Salvador to get Fuentes, and they agreed to join forces.

But Fuentes's troops had captured Lucy's brother, German, and two scouts while on a soft probe of the camp. Raven and Lucy were tasked with freeing her brother and the scouts. Raven's primary goal remained the same: kill Xavier Fuentes. If Lucy's reckless antics didn't get them both killed first...

WHEN THE ECHO of the rumbling trucks finally faded, Raven said, "Let's go." Lucy didn't argue. Both heard the countdown clock ticking. The main force of *El Tigre* fighters was coming up behind them.

Raven and Lucy crossed the rutted dirt road and advanced into the jungle. Raven's bandana felt soaked against his forehead.

They weren't worried about trip wires or mines as far from the camp as they were, but both looked for the telltale signs of each anyway. They were in no hurry. Leaves, branches, insects—all swatted, poked, or buzzed the pair as they progressed over the uneven terrain to the objective. Topping a rise prior to the final 25-yards to the camp perimeter, they took cover to watch. Gaps in the trees helped them see a section of the Fuentes camp.

The narco-terrorist facility sat in the V-notch of a mountain with the granite tower at its rear. Raven had ruled out an attack from the rear because of the mountain. Whoever designed the camp's layout liked tents and stacked tires. Each tent had a row of tires in front and on each side, about eight high by Raven's count. Good for cover and catching debris and stray bullets.

Raven focused on the large tent in the center of the camp rather than the smaller tents lining the outer edges. Fuentes would be in the command tent. The front flap was rolled up, leaving only three sides of the tent closed. With a pair of binoculars, Raven examined the men inside. They stood around a folding table. He tried to find Fuentes within the cluster of men.

Back corner. The narco-terrorist used frequent hand gestures as he explained something to another man, who appeared skeptical. He focused on Fuentes's face. Big, dark eyes; animated mouth; thin mustache. A camouflage cap matching his uniform concealed Fuentes's thick hair. His uniform looked tailored to his muscled frame.

The second man was older than Fuentes, and looked less uncertain the longer Fuentes spoke. The second man was taller, and had to look down at Fuentes; his short stature did not seem to bother the narco-terrorist.

A third man broke off from the activity at the center of the table to join them. Raven muttered, "Uh huh," and lowered the binoculars.

"What?" Lucy said.

"One of the people Fuentes saw at the nightclub is there."

"We have to find those trucks," she told him. They left the rise and followed the perimeter, staying 25 yards from the edge of the camp. This time, they moved much slower than before, and kept watch for traps.

They stumbled across none and presently stopped to observe the west side of the camp.

The trucks sat parked single file, with enough space between for men in camouflage to unload the cargo. Other troops stood and watched. The men who had ridden in the trucks did all the work. They unloaded crates from each truck, stacking them nearby, and nobody moved to open them. It seemed like a routine delivery, but with Fuentes talking to clients in the command tent, Raven knew the munitions delivery was destined for whatever job the client had in mind.

Complications kept building. Get Lucy's brother. Kill Fuentes. Now, blow the crates and whack the client.

I'm not sure twenty guys will be enough, Raven thought.

And then the unloading crew climbed back aboard the trucks. The engines rumbled to life. The vehicles began moving forward, following a path through the camp to...an unseen exit? Raven wasn't sure what to make of the development.

"Are they leaving?" Lucy whispered.

"Listen a moment," he said.

As Raven focused on the loud engines, camp troops began moving the crates, lifting them up high enough to place on wheeled carts. Others pulled the carts across the camp to a large square-shaped tent. The tent had a full wall of stacked tires around it, and the crew had little difficulty getting the bigger crates through the gap in front. Raven watched and frowned. Their armory? He filed the tent away as a secondary target.

Then the engines of the three trucks faded naturally. They did not relocate to another area of the camp.

"I think they left for good," Raven said.

"Still no sign of the prisoners," she said.

Raven took out his binoculars for another scan.

The row of tents to the left of the center tent stretched back toward the V-notch, but overgrowth forced a 90-degree turn. Tire stacks prevented him from seeing all but a couple of tents after the turn, but he found what he wanted. Three men in one of the tents sat with hands tied behind their backs. Dark welts covered their faces; dried blood caked on exposed skin; their camo uniforms were torn and splattered with more blood. Raven handed the binoculars to Lucy and told her where to look. She did.

"It's them."

Raven checked his watch. Five minutes till the *El Tigre* attack force arrived. They had to work fast around the perimeter and get close to the prisoners.

It can never be easy.

Lucy handed back the binoculars. "Why are they still alive?"

"Fuentes is planning another strike. He can leave the bodies of your brother and the other two at the scene and *El Tigre* takes the blame."

"We have to reach them." Lucy moved before Raven hissed, "Wait!" and was two steps ahead when her right foot snapped a tripwire.

RAVEN EXPECTED a bomb to go off in his face. Nothing exploded. Instead, he saw Lucy sprawled on the ground, dirt stuck to her face as she tried to rise. A portion of the trip-wire remained wrapped around her right boot. Raven pulled the wire free and followed the length through heavy leaves to the tree trunk. The wire didn't connect with a grenade or Claymore; instead, it connected to a black electronic box strapped to the base of the trunk. A red light flashed.

Lucy said, "Is it a dud?"

"No. Sensors. They know we're here."

Lucy cursed and scrambled to her feet, grabbing her fallen rifle. Her hands gripped the weapon as she scanned for threats. Raven tucked his own AK into his shoulder and said, "We gotta go. Now!"

Lucy still looked dazed from her fall, but Raven gave her a shove. She started forward, Raven behind her, and then they both stopped short.

Dogs barked. Low growls mixed with higher-pitched wails. Dogs, running. The enemy wasn't simply sending troops; the dogs would sniff out their hiding spots no matter how well they concealed themselves.

Raven grabbed Lucy's arm and they ran back the way they'd come. The strike force had to be less than three minutes out, but it might as well have been an eternity.

Raven grabbed Lucy and pulled her to cover. "What now?" she snapped.

"If we run too far your brother won't make it."

The barking grew louder. Men's voices joined the noise as they encouraged the dogs. Raven plucked a grenade from his vest and pulled the pin. He did not throw the grenade, but instead gestured for Lucy to do the same. She nodded as she caught the drift of his thinking and pulled the pin on her own hand-held explosive. Raven waited until he spotted the foliage ahead shifting as the enemy party neared. He tossed his grenade. It flew high and dropped out of sight. Lucy added hers. They dropped into the dirt. The twin blasts shook the ground. The dogs stopped barking. The men stopped talking. Raven raised his head. Smoke drifted around them.

He helped Lucy to her feet and they advanced toward the

camp once again. Their boots pounded the ground as they ran without slowing. Sudden explosions began within the camp, loud blasts - the artillery from the strike force landing on target. They ran faster.

THE MORTAR SHELLS arched over the camp and fell through the opening in the trees to hit the ground with devastating effect. The bombs tore chunks out of the ground and exploded tents into balls of fire, men running, screaming as shrapnel cut into them, the formerly quiet camp now in chaos. Those who survived the barrage took up defensive positions, but with the smoke thick and tents burning, they found their view of intruders obscured. And then machine guns opened up from within the jungle, somewhere outside the perimeter, unseen, but their effect very much the same as the overhead shells. Bullets cut down camouflaged fighters who returned fire in vain prior to their sudden end.

The *El Tigre* commandos broke through the outer line. The fight became a free-for-all as men clashed hand-to-hand or with guns. Bodies fell on both sides; others ran for better positions.

Raven ran through the fray, tossing a grenade into the tent where he'd seen troops deposit the crates. He and Lucy ran on. The explosion turned the tent into a flaming hulk of canvas. Ammunition inside began to cook off, stray bullets flying in all directions with popping sounds announcing their launch.

Raven and Lucy reached the tent with the three prisoners. Raven ducked inside with his AK-103 at the ready; no guards. When German saw his sister, he let out a yell of delight. The other two scouts, and their stunned expressions, contemplated her with brightening eyes after days of torture left them numb.

Raven and Lucy cut the bonds holding the prisoners' wrists together. The gunfire and explosions throughout the camp hammered their ears; nobody tried to talk. They helped the prisoners to their feet and exited with Raven in the lead. He checked for threats, then led his party to the right, between two other tents. He wanted to reach the jungle as fast as possible and send Lucy and the others on their way. He still had a job to finish.

They reached the jungle. German and the two scouts moved better than Raven thought they would. Thank the blood rush of rescue, renewed hope that they hadn't reached the end of the road, he decided.

Raven handed his Kalashnikov and spare ammo to German when they stopped. "Take these and get to the rendezvous."

"Where do you think you're going?" Lucy snapped.

"Taking care of Fuentes. Get your brother and his men out of here. I'll join you at the base camp."

"Raven—"

"Get her out of here," Raven snapped to German, who grabbed his sister. Lucy continued her protest before giving up and leading the three men along the pre-planned escape route.

Raven snatched the Nighthawk Custom Talon .45 autoloader from his right hip. He ran back into the fight. Smoke from the burning tents was thicker now, the shooting still intense, the screams of the dying and wounded filling the air as he sought the command tent in the middle of the fray.

Most of the fighting remained on the east and southern sides of the camp. Raven encountered no resistance, pausing at a tire stack to take stock of what was happening around him. *El Tigre* wanted blood; they were taking it from the Fuentes forces. The smoke stung Raven's eyes. Leaving the tire stack, he covered the last ten yards to the command tent and ran inside.

The men hiding behind an upturned table took a second to recognize Raven as an invader. His white face probably startled them more than anything, he realized, as he brought up the .45 and the other two raised automatic rifles. He fired twice. One gunner fell back with an extra hole between his eyes, the second felt his nose pushed through the back of his head by the .45 hollow-point before he lost consciousness forever. Raven turned to his right to check for more threats; he saw none. He also found no other sign of life in the tent. Fuentes and his clients may have fled, but they left behind computer equipment and maps. All good intel for *El Tigre* at a later date. But Raven didn't have time to look over the info. He had to find Fuentes.

Raven stowed the .45 and helped himself to a HK rifle and ammunition. The dead man loosely clutching the rifle wasn't going to need it any longer.

RAVEN FIRED at a Fuentes gunner aiming at an *El Tigre* machine gunner. The bullet hit the gunman in the neck and brought him down. He fired at another nearby who turned to look behind him; this time, the burst from the HK bored into the gunner's chest. Another down. Raven dropped behind a stack of tires to look around. The battle continued, but *El Tigre* seemed to have neutralized most of the enemy threat. What he didn't see was Fuentes himself, or the two clients from the command tent. In the smoke and mass of fighting bodies, it was impossible to identify faces. For all he knew, Fuentes was already dead, killed early in the fight, but with no body, Raven had to keep looking.

Where had the trucks gone? He looked around. When he spotted the beginning of the tire tracks, he followed the trail as far as he could. They led into the jungle. A grenade blast detonated near him, but the tires took the worst of the blast.

Rifle in hand, Raven ran, staying low, firing bursts at stray Fuentes fighters to keep them down. More shouting now—from *El Tigre* gunners demanding survivors lay down their weapons. Their fight was almost over, but Raven's remained in progress.

He followed the tracks into the trees. But he wasn't back in the jungle with the fight fading behind him. He entered a clearing, circular, where a line of ATVs sat. Across from them, a row of Jeeps with a gap suggesting one was missing. Raven ran to the nearest ATV. Keys waited in each ignition. He slung the rifle and mounted the ATV, twisting the key, kick-starting the motor. The little machine coughed to life with a puff of black exhaust smoke spurting out of the back. Raven popped the clutch and sped into the jungle, following a well-traveled path with fresh tire tracks. This was dangerous; he had no idea what he actually faced, but he couldn't allow Fuentes to breathe another day. If he died in the final confrontation, so be it; he long ago accepted his life ran on borrowed time.

He eased off the throttle. The path curved and twisted through the jungle, the trees and foliage making it hard to see more than a few feet ahead. Raven kept his head low to avoid hanging branches—the drawback of being tall.

The path finally straightened and the Jeep lay ahead. Raven increased speed, and the Jeep grew in size as he caught up. The passenger in back saw him, but instead of opening fire with a gun, he turned to the driver to shout the warning. Had Fuentes taken off with the clients but no firepower?

Time to find out. Raven held the left handlebar with a light grip and grabbed the .45 from side leather. He extended the gun and fired once, twice, a third shot—the back window didn't shatter; the slugs only bounced off, each round leaving only a shallow gouge in the bulletproof material.

He put the .45 away and unslung the rifle, then had to hold tight and steer with one hand as another curve appeared. Raven lost sight of the Jeep for a moment, but lined up with the vehicle again on the next straight. But another curve loomed ahead. He had to act fast.

He braced the rifle on the handlebars and flipped the selector switch for full-auto. *Let's see how the tires hold up.* Raven fired one burst; a miss. Dirt flew up behind the tires. He raised the barrel a little and fired another burst, then held back the trigger until the magazine ran dry. As the HK's action locked back, Raven saw his reward.

The two tires in the rear blew under the impact of the HK's 5.56mm rounds, the back end of the Jeep sinking to drag in the dirt. The off-roader slowed. Raven swung the ATV off the path and jumped off, dropping to use the little four-wheeler for cover as he slapped home a new mag into the HK and then his pistol. The Jeep had stopped; the doors opened and two men—the clients—leaped out. They fired a pair of pistol shots and the rounds whistled pat Raven. He didn't have a clear shot. With the Nighthawk .45 holstered and the HK at the ready, Raven swung around the back of the ATV and onto the path. He sighted and fired. The younger of the two clients pitched backwards as Raven's rounds cut into him. Raven dived left into the foliage as return fire came his way. The older client approached, screaming obscenities; Raven plugged him between the eyes, and the man's body flopped in the center of the path.

Raven left the concealment of the leaves and ran to the Jeep. As he reached the bumper, Fuentes tried to shoot around the front fender. Raven dodged back before the narco-terrorist pulled the trigger, and the shots flew wide. With a yell, Fuentes bolted for the thick jungle on his right. Raven shouldered the HK. Before the jungle swallowed Fuentes again, Raven eased back on the trigger. The HK bucked against his shoulder; the 5.56mm tumblers ripped open Fuentes's back. Fuentes only let out a short scream. Momentum carried him forward until his body smacked a tree trunk. He bounced off the trunk and landed on the jungle floor.

Raven cautiously approached the fallen body. He had to make sure. He found Fuentes on his back, his face frozen in a tightened grimace, eyes still open, but the bloody holes covering his chest and blood pooling on the ground told Raven all he needed to know. Fuentes was dead. Mission accomplished.

TWENTY-FOUR HOURS LATER, in a tuxedo with a white dinner jacket, Raven sat in the bar of a fancy restaurant wondering if Lucy Pinto was going to show, or stand him up.

Yes, he'd asked her to leave in the middle of the fight, to get her brother and the two scouts to safety. She had her mission, he had his; he misjudged her investment in *his*, and she didn't appreciate him sending her away. Upon their reunion after the battle, she'd made her point of view clear:

"You ass!"

He was too tired to argue, which didn't slow her down, and she continued to let him know about her displeasure on the truck ride back to the *El Tigre* base. When Raven packed up to return to the city and his hotel, he invited her to join him at the hotel restaurant. She said she'd never sit with him in a restaurant, or anywhere else, ever again. He gave her the address and his room number and a preferred time anyway. She told him, "I hope you choke on your martini olive!" But she'd also snatched the piece of paper upon which he wrote the details out of his hand.

Raven ate the olive in his martini, and did not choke. But he did wonder if Lucy meant what she said as he watched the entrance. Patrons entered and exited; none of them were Lucy Pinto. *She can't stay mad forever; then again...*

Raven grinned as memories of other fiery warriors like Lucy came to mind. Some remained alive; some hadn't survived; others he'd made sure never to see again because he knew, deep down, he didn't want to leave them. But the rules he lived by made sure he never stayed in one place for too long. In fact, no longer than necessary to get a job done. There were other jobs to do, other victims; his war had no end. Peace was for others, not him.

He swallowed more of his martini and savored the taste of the gin. His secret to a good martini would send other aficionados into the stratosphere with indignation. Raven liked to add a teaspoon of water after the pour. The extra water cut down on the alcohol smell and taste, and brought out the natural flavors of the gin (or vodka, if one insisted on ruining a martini). The only drawback was how easy it became to forget the ingestion of a large amount of alcohol; the trick made "Give me another" an easy phrase, but before long the unsuspecting enthusiast found themselves unable to walk without support, and felt like hell the next morning.

Raven knew from experience.

Sometimes, he let it happen on purpose. But now wasn't one of those times.

He set the glass down and observed the restaurant. He felt like the only one alone, which made him self-conscious. He wondered if he was destined to watch others enjoy life while he scrambled for meaning behind his existence other than war without end.

And then Lucy walked in.

Raven sighed. He hadn't liked where his thoughts were going, and her appearance turned his mind to much more pleasant ponderings. He raised a hand. She crossed the restaurant to the bar. Her long white dress had no straps at the shoulders; she filled out the fabric very well, with her long hair down at her shoulders in a cascading wave. She'd gone light on the makeup, and she smiled when she reached him.

"I didn't choke on my olive," he announced.

She shook her head. "I don't know why I'm here. I *should* still be mad."

"I wanted you and your brother to get to safety. Wasn't he your goal?"

"I had more than one."

The bartender came over and she ordered a glass of white wine. "Do you have a table reserved?"

"Upper dining room," he said.

"Big assumption considering you might have been there alone."

"Oh, I'd have found another companion." He grinned. She scowled. Her wine arrived and she swallowed a mouthful.

"How is your brother?"

"Banged up, but he will live."

"Good."

"You have become a legend in *El Tigre*," Lucy said, "the gringo commando who took out Fuentes and two other men without hesitation. No wonder you're so vain. You think you can do anything."

"Sure," Raven said. "I can even make you calm down instead of being a bitch."

She slapped a hand on the bar. "You will take that back."

Raven kept his eyes on hers. If anybody was watching the drama, he didn't notice. He knew what she was doing, but had to fight to keep a grin from tugging at either side of his mouth.

RAVEN AND LUCY had their clothes half off before Raven had shut the hotel room door. He threw her onto the bed and she dug her nails into his back as he landed on top of her. He hadn't been wrong; she hadn't been mad, but looking to stir up drama for some of the best make-up sex either had ever had.

Later, as she lay on "her side" of the bed snoring, Raven slipped out and pulled on a bathrobe. He wanted to pack quickly, albeit quietly as well, in order to be at the airport early. When the nightstand lamp snapped on as he opened the top drawer of the dresser, he froze.

"What are you doing?"

"Go back to sleep."

"Are you leaving?"

"I'm packing."

"Why are you packing?" she said.

"I'm leaving in the morning, Lucy."

"It *is* morning."

"Later."

He filled his suitcase with shirts and socks as she flung the cover off. He heard her feet scraping on the carpeted floor as she approached.

She wrapped bare arms around him and pressed the rest of her naked body against his backside. "Are you sure you want to go?" She snaked her hands under the front of the robe and ran fingernails along his stomach.

He felt the warmth of her body through the robe, and the

heat of her hands as they explored, but staying longer? No. He had to get moving again. He shook her away.

"Hey!"

He turned and stroked the right side of her face before giving her a kiss. "I'm sorry. I can't stay."

"Can't? Or won't?"

"Both."

She cursed at him and pulled away. She sat on her side of the bed with her shoulders slumped. It wasn't a good look for her without any clothes on, but he didn't say so. Raven returned to his task and filled his suitcase. Zipping it closed, he set it beside the closet.

"Why won't you stay with me?" she said.

"There are others like you, Lucy. They need me."

It wasn't the life he'd wanted. Raven had seen the worst the world had to offer and escaped for a quiet civilian life. Then fate dealt a cruel blow with sudden tragedy, and vengeance became his new mission. The only link to his past was the sterling silver locket around his neck, which currently rested on the nightstand, and Lucy hadn't asked why he wore it. He never talked about what the locket contained, but it motivated his crusade. He pursued the world's predators, those who created victims and heartache, to deliver justice one bullet at a time.

"But I need you more!"

"You can take care of yourself."

"Speaking in double meanings now, Raven?"

He wasn't in the mood for joking. He didn't want to leave, but he knew too well the consequences of staying. Rule One: No Roots. He wasn't going to break it again. Never again.

"At least come back to bed," she said. "Sun doesn't come up for a few hours."

"All right."

She snuggled beside him once he returned to the warm bed. He tried to sleep, but only stared at the ceiling.

OLIVER KOHLBERG SWISHED COGNAC IN A SNIFTER AND DRANK down a mouthful of the delicious elixir. He stood on the balcony overlooking the front of his estate. He was on the front balcony; he had another in the back. He wanted the view of the front this time. It was a warm day with a gentle breeze and he had the conference room prepared for arriving guests. Others planned to attend via video.

In his youth, Kohlberg cut a dashing figure; six-three, athletic, the bane of lesser men when it came to attracting women. Age had ruined him. At 85, he stood with a hunch, his body toting more weight than he liked, his hair white and thinning. But he hadn't wasted his time. He might be accused of letting himself go many years ago, which brought him to his current state, but he had a goal, and he worked toward the goal at the expense of everything else. He was closer than ever to achieving what he'd set out to do decades ago: reshape the globe in his own image.

Armed guards wandered the grounds below. He lived with a target on his back and rarely ventured outside the estate. While he had more allies than enemies, factions of the enemy camp wanted him dead. But he had made arrangements to make sure not even death, natural or otherwise, halted his plans.

Movement far ahead caught his eyes. He squinted. A car sat at the main gate. His guards were there with hand-held mirrors checking under the car for bombs. Dogs sniffed for other dangers; once his men confirmed the party in the car was indeed expected, they'd be allowed through the gate. Kohlberg checked his watch. They were five minutes early. Having been to the estate before, his guests had allowed time for the security check. They knew he appreciated—no, *demanded*—promptness.

His estate sprawled before him, full of green grass, trees, ponds, a paradise on earth. He liked nature and didn't fill the property with extra structures. The main house contained everything he needed and his employees required. The open space also helped his defensive measures. An attacking force had nowhere to hide; caught in the open, they'd be easy targets for his countermeasures.

Somebody behind him said, "Herr Kohlberg."

He turned. His chief of security, Hanno, stood in a partially open French door. "They are here," he added.

"Do not delay them any longer," Kohlberg said in his deep voice. "Escort them to the conference room. I will arrive shortly."

Hanno nodded and went away.

Presently Kohlberg watched the main gate swing open and the car travel along the access road to the front of the house. He did not wave as the car drew closer. But he did watch with a grim stare. He wasn't one to smile, even on the cusp of victory. He still had too much work to do, and when victory finally arrived, even more work.

His final plan was in full operation. Once complete, the world would never be the same. He'd never considered failure, now or in the past. There were missteps, delays, complications, setbacks, all expected problems and solved over the course of time. He liked to tell his people problems didn't matter.

"Nothing can stop what is coming," he'd tell them. "*Nothing*."

THE WOMAN ASKED, "Is he standing on the balcony?"

Arthur Hunt, behind the wheel of the rented white Volkswagen, turned briefly to grin at the excited face of Emma Bell. The young woman's eyes were wide with anticipation. This was her first time meeting the man who had only been an image on a screen or photograph for so long. Yet she'd taken his orders and followed instructions like the best of soldiers in any army.

"It is," Hunt said. "Don't wave. He won't acknowledge us."

"Right," Emma said. "Super serious. Laser focused." She recalled her briefing with Hunt prior to the trip. She needed to remember to keep her mouth shut until Kohlberg asked for input; he didn't tolerate having his meetings full of chatter on top of chatter. Butterflies fluttered in her stomach and she tried to calm down with a series of deep breaths. She had nothing to fear. She had performed her duties in service of the Fraternity to the letter, and would do so till the end. But the idea of facing the grim face of her leader made Emma mentally check off everything she'd done so far in hopes he found no flaw in her work.

It's not about you, she chided herself. It wasn't as if she'd been summoned for a personal audience. This was an all-hands meeting to discuss the final phase of the plan; still, she felt anxious.

Emma glanced at Hunt. If he shared any of her internal reactions, he hid it well. *Best poker face ever*, she thought.

The house grew larger as they approached. Armed men pointed to a parking space beside the porch. Hunt followed the silent instructions and stopped the car where directed. The guards stayed a few feet away. As Arthur Hunt and Emma Bell exited, another man walked over. He carried no weapons.

"My name is Hanno," he said. "I am the head of security. Welcome to Herr Kohlberg's home. Please follow me."

Hunt collected his briefcase from the back of the car. A guard moved in fast. He snatched the case away and kneeled on the ground. The guard inspected the contents, pawed through the pockets, checked documents and asked Emma if she had anything. She showed him her empty hands.

"Enough," Hanno snapped. The guard closed the case and held it out for Hunt, who accepted it with a thank you.

"Follow me," Hanno said again.

Neither were used to taking orders. They commanded their own set of people, not part of the Fraternity, but instead part of the US intelligence community.

Arthur Hunt and Emma Bell worked for the CIA; they were part of the many tentacles Oliver Kohlberg had wormed into the governments of the world. As far as the Agency was concerned, they were both on separate vacations.

———————

ARTHUR HUNT LOOKED BACK to make sure Emma was with him. She trailed about a foot behind.

He wasn't worried about being spotted at the estate. Kohlberg was not under watch by any of the world's alphabet soup agencies. He was not listed among the bad actors who received the CIA's attention, either.

For all his life, Kohlberg had been in business. His companies invented and sold products to a variety of industries all over the globe. It was how he'd begun his influence. Now, as a billionaire several times over, he dedicated his time to charitable efforts and political organizations, promoting chosen candidates throughout the world. His candidates often won, though they did so less by the public actually *choosing* said candidate and more by manipulating vote totals where necessary. How? He owned the companies that supplied the electronic voting machines. He knew the ins and outs of each country and how to exploit their weaknesses. His people at the scene did the rest. Kohlberg thought big and small. Having candidates win town and city elections who were loyal to him, and the plan, was as important as installing Senators and Presidents. All the cogs worked together for the benefit of the overall machine.

Kohlberg had his enemies, yes, a small number who understood his endgame. But they had to fight on *his* playing field. Outright assassination would be seen for what it was: murder. He was not an overt threat, but made his moves in the shadows and hidden corners and through representatives with no visible connection to him. He'd worked hard to learn how to protect himself. The protections helped assure Arthur Hunt that he had no danger in appearing as ordered. Some conversations needed to take place face-to-face.

Hunt's concerns centered on his own family, and keeping them from discovering his double life. The CIA thought he was fishing; his family thought he was on yet another official trip for the government. He'd taken many such trips over the years. The lies came easy because he couldn't talk about his work. Only his wife knew he worked for the CIA. His kids believed he was an art curator at the Smithsonian.

The security chief, Hanno, showed them into a large room with a long table. "Take a seat." They did so. Leather folders sat in front of them. Neither made a move to open the folders or touch the water pitchers. Hanno stood near the door.

The room was quiet.

Almost like a tomb.

2

THE DOOR SWUNG OPEN. OLIVER KOHLBERG ENTERED. HE snapped, "Leave us," to Hanno, who departed and shut the door behind him.

"Welcome," Kohlberg stated without warmth. He paused at the head of the table. He didn't sit, but instead lifted a remote and aimed at the wall facing the table. The rows of mounted wide-screen monitors brightened, but of the eight, only seven faces appeared on each screen. The last remained blank.

"Thank you for being on time," Kohlberg said. He glanced at the faces on the screens, but settled last on Hunt and Emma. "We have an issue to discuss, even as our forces move into position and await action orders. Please open the folders in front of you."

Hunt and Emma did so. Kohlberg watched them examine the single photo inside. The men on the monitors, made up of various nationalities, looked down. Kohlberg knew none of them had opened the folders he'd sent early, because he had every single member of his group under constant visual and audio surveillance. They had no idea his prying eyes intruded into their private lives.

Kohlberg continued. "You'll notice the photograph is of one of our members. Mr. Philip Weigel. He's not here, because he's no longer part of this organization."

Kohlberg paused. Nobody asked questions. All eyes focused on him. He notices faces full of concern from those who'd known Weigel.

"Mr. Weigel has a case of cold feet, and informed me he no longer wanted to be part of our efforts. But this is where our problem lies. He knows too much, but we can't murder him. Like some of us, he is a public figure. His death may bring more trouble than we need. The question we face is what to do about him, and I called this meeting to ask your input."

Kohlberg clasped his hands behind his back, which made his jutting belly more prominent. "We shall now discuss." He called on each member of the Fraternity; they offered opinions and ideas. Hunt and Emma offered their own suggestions. The meeting did not get loud; nobody spoke over another. Kohlberg made sure his meetings remained orderly at all times.

In the end, all agreed their former associate had an Achilles heel: his wife.

A simple plan developed. Grab the wife for the duration of their final phase. Her disappearance would force Weigel to keep his mouth shut as long as she remained in danger.

Hunt raised a hand.

"Yes, Arthur," Kohlberg said.

"How do we know he hasn't leaked information already?"

Kohlberg shook his head. "We can hear him breathing. If he has spoken, I'd know. We need to keep him quiet as events begin to advance."

"We have people who can handle the situation," Hunt said.

"That pleases me greatly," Kohlberg said. "You have the assignment. Do not fail."

HUNT DROVE the Audi out the front gate, turned left, and began driving back the way they'd come.

He had to settle his own nerves. Agreeing to carry out the Weigel kidnapping was a tall order.

"Price can do it."

Hunt looked sharply at Emma. It was as if she'd read his mind.

"Good idea," Hunt said. "His work organizing the cells is done. He's idle right now."

"He's an amazing man," Emma said.

"Price?"

"No, Kohlberg. Did you see how he commanded everybody's attention?"

"Too many times. Look, about Price. You're his handler, so do you want to reach out and make contact?"

"Of course."

Hunt caught a gleam in her eye as he faced the road again.

LESLIE WEIGEL WAS USED to the spotlight. Today's speech was another in a long time of speeches she'd given in the last twelve months, and she'd only changed her script a little. Anybody coming to see her for a second time might remember some of her words from before.

Her driver parked curbside in front of the hospital and stopped. She stepped out into the hot afternoon air as a man and woman approached to greet her. She'd left her jacket at the hotel because of the 85-degree afternoon.

"Hello, Mrs. Weigel," said the man. She had to think fast to remember his name. Luckily, it didn't take long.

"William, so happy to see you." She shook his hand with a weak grip. The custom was one she wasn't good at. She turned to the woman, somebody older like her named Pamela, and shook hands with her, too, as they exchanged greetings.

"The press is out in force, my goodness," Leslie Weigel said, glancing over William and Pamela's shoulders at the crowd near the hospital doors. They aimed cameras in her direction. The press was a disagreeable part of her job, but a necessary one, and part of the reason her husband Philip never attended her ribbon-cutting events.

She was in Miami to cut the ribbon on a new children's wing of one of the city's hospitals, and give a short speech about the better healthcare Miami's kids would receive thanks to the new wing. William and Pamela, hospital executives, guided her toward the crowd of media. She'd forgotten their exact positions at the hospital, but had been working with them since construction of the wing began.

Leslie Weigel and her husband had helped fund the new wing via their charitable foundation, but they were silent donors—they would not have the wing named after them. The thought hadn't crossed their minds to ask for such an honor. It was enough to help, to give back something to others since they'd been so successful with their business ventures.

Leslie spoke with the reporters for two minutes, reciting a prepared and memorized statement of thanks and gratitude to the city and the hospital for making the new wing happen; she added platitudes about helping local kids, and was happy not to flub her lines. It wasn't as if she didn't care, but she found no real value in talking about things. *Doing* mattered more. Getting the children's wing built was the prize; the attention which followed, and forced her to engage in PR work when she'd rather not, was simply part of the process she'd come to accept, but also despised. But she didn't despise it enough to avoid the effort entirely. Unlike her husband. Showing up and speaking kept the Weigel Foundation in the public eye, which in turn brought more opportunities to give back. It wasn't a horrible trade-off.

William took her by the elbow and moved to the entrance, the press parting to let her through, and then they were inside where peace and silence continued to elude. Another crowd waited, this one made up of city officials, other donors, and local rich folks who'd accepted the exclusive invite to attend the opening ceremony and fund-rising lunch. Leslie shook hands and exchanged greetings with more people she didn't know, went blank on faces she recognized, and made her cheeks hurt with a constant smile. *Think of the kids*, she reminded herself. *Also, learn names better.*

She felt relieved when they finally took her inside the hospital conference room where the audience waited. William and Pamela escorted her to the stage with its traditional podium and microphone.

She wished they were holding the ceremony outside the entrance to the children's wing, but there were too many people to fit in the small hallway leading to the doors of the new addition. After her speech, she'd spend the next few hours taking groups for a tour so they could witness what their money purchased.

She gave a mercifully short speech, not for the crowd, but for her. As she wrapped, Leslie decided William and Pamela's joint introduction of her went longer than her speech. The three of them rotated giving tours of the new wing, and by the time Leslie climbed back into her car, she let her driver know she was officially tapped out for the day.

"Straight back to the hotel, sounds nice," the driver said.

His name was Blake. He'd been her household driver for at least six years. Leslie had come to depend on him even on her trips. He was a calming presence amidst the chaos of mixing with so many strangers. As nice as William and Pamela had been, and everybody else, she doubted she'd ever see them again. *Onto the next...*

"Yes, Blake, as fast as traffic allows, please."

Blake drove off.

Leslie Weigel leaned back in her seat and closed her eyes.

When she opened her eyes thirty minutes later, she didn't recognize where Blake was taking her. All she knew was they were nowhere near the hotel.

"Blake?"

Her driver said nothing. He pressed a switch on the dash. The plastic divider between front and back separated the pair as it rose to meet the roof. She yelled his name again as a thin cloud of white gas hissed through the rear A/C vents. Leslie Weigel gasped and choked but quickly fell unconscious. Blake waited a few minutes, then turned off the gas. Little by little, the gaps in the window frames allowed the gas to escape. Blake continued driving. They had a long way to go yet.

3

SAM RAVEN SAT IN THE DARK BAR AND WAITED FOR HIS contact. He was in Naples, Florida, and wouldn't have agreed to the meeting if he'd been going straight home to Stockholm. But he had decided to swing through the US after leaving El Salvador. He wasn't in a hurry to get home.

He drank more of his Old Fashioned and watched the front door. A woman was coming to collect him and bring him to the potential client, who, for some reason, did not want to go out in public. It was nothing new to Raven. The people who reached out to him often worked through representatives and middle-men; nature of the business.

Raven had one clue about the job. They wanted him to transport a package from one point to another without asking questions. Raven had been tempted to joke he wasn't "the transport guy" but the grimness of the caller's tone suggested the humor might be lost. They promised him thirty thousand US dollars simply for taking the meeting. What the hell, right? Thirty K was thirty K.

He enjoyed the quiet bar while he waited. The tavern catered to an older clientele, and the buzz of conversation wasn't overpowering. Raven still understood his own thoughts. He wanted the job not because he needed the money, but because he didn't want to go home right away. There was nothing at home to return to—except an empty houseboat. There were consequences to living by the rules he'd pledged to abide by, to nobody but himself, and lately he'd become more sensitive to the consequences than before. He didn't want to go home, so it made sense to take a job. El Salvador had been a freebie. He could say he needed to make up the money he'd spent chasing Xavier Fuentes, but he wasn't capable of lying to himself. He was lonely, and action was as good a companion as any, and he *always* encountered interesting people when on a job. Most of the time, they were the bad guys and he shot them; but there were exceptions, too.

Keeping the war chest full came with its own benefit. The money allowed him to fight his war without end the way the ghosts of his past demanded.

Anyway, it was too late to say no. He'd already accepted the initial terms.

But how long did they expect him to wait?

He finished his drink and asked for a refill. When the waiter delivered, Raven checked his watch. She was fifteen minutes late. He sipped the drink. If she didn't arrive by the time he finished, he'd walk away.

Raven checked his phone. He examined the picture of his contact the client had sent so he'd recognize her. Her name was Erika. Red hair, thin face, green eyes. The headshot showed her without makeup; she looked generic, like any two dozen women he might pass on the street without a second glance. He wondered who the client was and what he truly represented. Generic faces had plenty of value when you didn't want anybody to notice you.

He put the phone away inside his sport coat, took another

sip of his Old Fashioned, and watched the door. When she finally entered, he couldn't help but raise an eyebrow and watch for reactions from other men nearby. The men remained absorbed in their conversations. She was invisible.

Erika had committed to the role. Her long hair looked uncombed, as if she'd released it from a bun or pony tail only seconds before; her blouse and skirt combo showed the day's use via strategic wrinkles. She carried black pumps in her left hand and wore tennis shoes. She was an overworked nobody secretary at the end of a long day.

Erika smiled at Raven as she joined him, dropping into the chair opposite with an exaggerated sigh. The pumps *clopped* onto the floor as she released them.

"I need a drink," she announced. And winked at him.

"Impressive," Raven said. He raised a hand to get the waiter's attention as he passed, but the fellow missed the signal and stopped to tend to another table. Raven waited.

"We appreciate you coming," Erika said.

"You're late."

"Had to make sure nobody followed me. I'm sure you understand."

"I understand thirty grand and a simple task," Raven said. Before she replied, the waiter passed again and this time Raven grabbed his attention. She asked for a gin-and-tonic with a twist of lime peel.

Raven continued. "If you have to watch your six, it sounds like this job isn't simple. I'd like to know about the complications if I'm going to carry out the instructions."

"It's not as bad as it sounds. My boss simply wants precautions taken to make sure a small problem doesn't turn into a crisis."

The waiter brought her drink; she and Raven clinked glasses.

"Where is your boss?"

"A few blocks away in a hotel room. We'll take my car if it's okay with you."

"I prefer we take mine."

"No argument. We don't want you uncomfortable, Mr. Raven."

Raven gave her a weak smile. He hadn't taken off his sport coat because he wore his gun in a speed rig underneath. The pistol hung close to his torso under his left arm. Ready for trouble. But he hoped they didn't face a problem requiring him to shoot their way out.

A hotel was a public place, and Raven lived by two rules.

The first, no roots. Nothing to tie him to one place or any person. He'd learned the hard way what happened when he allowed comfort and complacency into his life.

The second, no gunfights in public. If he had to fight, he wanted to steer clear of innocent bystanders. He worked to protect, not create more victims.

He hoped the client's problems didn't come calling, and he wasn't walking into a trap. He'd battled many enemies over the years. Some had survived despite his best efforts to end their lives. He was well aware they might someday catch up to him.

Erika downed her gin-and-tonic in two long swallows. She set her glass down. "Shall we go?"

Raven left his drink unfinished. Erika took care of the tab and tip.

4

RAVEN LET ERIKA TAKE A SLIGHT LEAD AS THEY EXITED THE bar. They followed the sidewalk to the corner ahead. She kept her back and shoulders straight, purse and arms close to her body, the pumps tucked under her left arm. She moved her head back and forth as she scanned for danger. Raven looked for trouble, too, but his movements weren't as obvious. He didn't like the idea of the job coming with complications; he didn't want to get into a fight this early; or in the current environment. There were too many people around, too many cars. It was still rush hour at the end of the business day, and the noise was bad. He couldn't hear anybody coming up behind them. By the time the sound of a threat reached him, they'd be in the thick of a fight with no way out.

"See anybody?" Raven asked her.

"We're clear so far."

"I agree." He took her left elbow. "Turn left up here. I'm parked on the street."

He unlocked the Jaguar with the remote and opened the

passenger door for her. She dropped into the seat and placed her purse and pumps on the floor at her feet. He climbed in on his side, started the car, and lurched away from the curb with both hands on the wheel as soon as a break in traffic opened.

"Nice car."

"It's a rental," he said.

"I can see you like to live good even if you're only passing through."

"Who told you I was only passing through?"

"You aren't unknown to us, Mr. Raven. It's why we called you. You keep a low profile, but anybody who has ever had any dealings with you can discuss your habits."

Raven grunted. Habits weren't terrible, but they created patterns. Detectible, predictive patterns. He'd have to monitor himself and find a way to alter his actions.

The new client hadn't called him directly. The only way to reach Raven was through a middle man in Europe—a man named Oscar Morey, who was Raven's eyes and ears for potential jobs. Oscar was a former underworld figure who now worked the information stream. When Raven needed to know something, he called Oscar. When somebody wanted Raven for a job, they called Oscar, and Oscar called him to talk it over before forwarding Raven's number. It was a system designed to help Raven keep his backside covered. He wondered if it truly did any good if Erika's remarks had any truth to them.

You're being paranoid. Cool it.

"Where am I going?" he asked.

"No tails?" she said.

Raven laughed. He'd been checking, but with so much other traffic to monitor, he hadn't seen anybody *specifically* following them. He told her so.

"Make the next left," Erika said.

Raven switched to the left lane, slowed for the turn, and cleared the light between yellow and red.

ERIKA WALKED BRISKLY DOWN the quiet hotel hallway. Raven stayed behind her, senses on alert. He'd unbuttoned his sport coat for easy access to his gun in case he needed the weapon. He hoped not. And his rule applied—if he needed to draw, he'd swing the barrel at skulls before pulling the trigger. Stray bullets punched through walls.

Erika stopped at room 3006 and knocked. It wasn't a straight knock, but a series of taps, a code, but Raven still hung back two steps and turned his head in both directions in case he needed to boogey.

The lock clicked and the door opened. A big man in a black suit answered. He examined Erika, grunted; looked at Raven, and raised an eyebrow at Erika.

"He's the one," she said.

The big man opened the door all the way. Erika led Raven through. No other bodyguards. A man beyond middle age sat in a corner easy chair, face weathered with experience, but wearing a sharp suit with silk tie and brightly polished shoes. The client. The drapes covered the windows; the room was warm.

"Welcome, Mr. Raven. Thank you for seeing me."

"You know me. I don't know you."

"My name is Philip Weigel."

"Never heard of you."

"Good."

Weigel's thick black hair might have been colored, but the dye job was a good one. Mid-60s, Raven guessed. A few lines on his face, but in otherwise good shape. No padding under the chin or softness in the cheeks.

But Raven had indeed never heard of the man, and he asked Weigel where he was from.

"I live here in Florida. Not this city. My business interests are wide and varied and would surely bore you to tears. My wife and I are involved in a lot of charitable foundations, and we have our own, and if you read the papers or saw the news this morning you might have seen my wife at a ribbon cutting."

"I missed the morning editions," Raven said.

"No matter. All you need to know is the thirty grand is in cash, and you get it whether you take this job or not."

"I have a feeling this job has nothing to do with moving a simple package."

"Please listen before you decide. Yes, there is no package. I didn't, couldn't, take the risk of somebody learning why I *really* wanted you here, Mr. Raven."

Raven detected the change in Weigel's voice. A flutter, a nervous interruption in an otherwise calm demeanor.

"Got an extra chair?" Raven said.

WEIGEL SAID, "My wife's been taken." His voice cracked again. Raven had a feeling this was the first time he'd said the words out loud and verbally admitted the crisis. Weigel moved to conceal his right hand by covering it with his left. But that didn't stop the hand from shaking.

"Okay."

"I need you to help get her back."

"I can help, certainly. But I need details, Mr. Weigel. Who has her? Why? Do you know where she is? Stuff like that. Please continue."

Weigel looked at the carpet, shifted in his seat, and cast a quick glance at his silver Rolex. Raven noticed the man's Berluti shoes, black leather Oxfords. He was a man who had earned the money to buy a lot of nice things, but his wife was gone, and the money and nice things suddenly didn't mean as much. Raven had seen the pattern many times before, in many similar kidnap cases. And he hated making promises to recover missing loved ones because sometimes the worst-case scenario occurred. Raven would rather face a bullet in the head than hear a desperate mother shout, *"You promised!"* The trick was to make assurances without making promises.

He'd learned the hard way.

"As I said," Weigel continued, "she had a ribbon cutting yesterday. A hospital opened a new children's wing thanks to the efforts of our foundation, and others, too, but she had to be there because our group did most of the world. She was seen getting into her car at the end of the ceremony, but she never made it back to the hotel. I waited for her to come home, and she didn't. Instead, I received a phone call demanding a ransom and no police or FBI. Then I thought of you."

"How much do they want?"

"Two million. We have four days. When they get the money, they'll tell me where to find her."

"Uh-huh."

"You sound like you don't believe me."

"You didn't call me to investigate and search."

Erika, from her seat at the corner desk, said, "Just tell him."

Raven frowned. But he made no overt moves. He kept his legs crossed and arms folded as he sat in the chair near the bed. The bodyguard wasn't far away, and any sudden moves might inspire the big man to take action.

Philip Weigel sighed. "All right. I know where my wife is.

She's been taken to the Balkans, to a camp. I'm not sure which camp, but it's one of three possibilities, and honest mercenaries are hard to find, which is why I called you."

Weigel spoke in a rush and Raven had to strain to catch all the words.

"You want me to raid the camp your wife has been taken to."

"Yes."

"They moved her across the ocean really fast. How soon between the kidnapping and the phone call?"

"They called on a satellite phone, from a plane, on their way," Weigel said. "My wife told me she was on a jet."

"How do you know which area she's been taken to?"

Weigel glanced across at Erika.

The redhead said, "That's my area of expertise, Mr. Raven."

"You should apply at the NSA."

"They can't afford me."

"Me either," Raven said with a grin.

"Can you help?" Weigel said. "Erika will give you all the details."

"Count me in."

"Would you like the thirty thousand in cash or—"

"Cash is fine. I'll need it for down payments on the people I'll need to hire. As for my real fee—"

"Name it."

"Two million if I pull it off."

"If?"

"Nothing if I don't," Raven said.

Weigel's face turned white.

"It's a possibility you have to accept," Raven said. "But I will do everything I can to make sure I earn the two mill."

Weigel nodded sharply.

"All this," Raven said, looking around the room, "was to dodge the bad guys?"

"I think they bugged my home," Weigel said. "I need to check. But, yes, this place was safe."

Raven noted Weigel used the past tense.

5

RAVEN DROVE ERIKA BACK TO THE BAR, WHERE SHE collected her car. Before departing, she passed him a blank business card. She's scrawled the name of a hotel, a room number, and her cell number. "Noon, sharp, tomorrow," she'd said.

Raven took it easy on the way back to his own hotel. He let questions rattle around in his mind. He hoped Oscar was awake on his side of the world to provide a few answers.

Safely back in his hotel room, a cup of hot tea in hand, he sat and called Oscar. He reached the information ace on the third ring.

"You pick the strangest people for me to see, Oscar."

"Is there a problem?"

Raven related the story of the meeting, the guarded explanation of events, the eventual truth.

"Something isn't right. Weigel says I have the whole story, but it doesn't add up."

"What doesn't add up?"

"I'm not sure yet. It's a gut feeling. His wife was whisked overseas. Why? He also thinks his house is bugged. How could he know? Either she's been gone longer than he's said, or he knows more than he's told me."

"Why take the job then?"

"I'm a sucker."

"Seriously, do you need the money?"

"No, I don't need the money, but I don't want to go home yet either."

"Why?"

"Tired of spending time with my own reflection."

"Tell Weigel to shove it and come stay with me and the old lady for a few days."

Raven laughed. "I appreciate the offer, but your old lady would run me out of the house after one wild night with you."

"You really want to do this?"

"Weigel is hiding a lot, but he needs help. Whatever he's into, it's come to collect in a way he never expected. I want a rundown on who he is and what he's involved with, and who, and why he has a personal intelligence officer on the payroll."

"Got a name?"

"First name. Erika. She's the one who apparently located where the enemy took the wife, and judging by the timeline she'd have to be clairvoyant. She's another big question mark."

"Age of the internet, Sam," Oscar said. "Everything is fast now."

"Get me what you can and I'll call you back tomorrow. I'm meeting Erika at noon to learn more."

"Be careful."

"I will. I'm calling the usual suspects for help. I'll have plenty of backup if the pizza hits the fan."

They said good-bye and Raven sat alone with his tea. He stared at the floor with his lips pressed together and thought about the evening's events once again. Weigel said his wife's ribbon cutting had made the news. He wanted to learn more. He took out his cell phone from inside his sport jacket, and his hand brushed the butt of the .45 under his left arm. He shook his head. He was so used to the rig he forgot to take it off when he no longer required a weapon. He set down the tea and stood long enough to shed his coat and harness. Sitting with the phone again, he tapped the internet icon and searched for any news items relating to Leslie Weigel.

He found the story of the children's hospital wing ribbon cutting. "Huh," he said aloud. The cutting had indeed taken place twenty-four hours earlier. Perhaps the kidnappers had called Weigel while in the air, and Erika had somehow tracked their phone signal to their final destination. But to do so meant they'd expected the call and had equipment set up to intercept the signal. They knew Mrs. Weigel was missing before the kidnappers informed them.

More questions. What were they hiding?

And why the Balkans? He knew of no syndicate in the region actively targeting Americans, and if there was one, they'd target Americans already *there*, who were easy pickings. They wouldn't be trolling through the US to grab somebody and fly them across the ocean. They'd keep her local, close to the family...

Maybe Oscar has a point. Tell them to stick it and move on.

Raven put the phone and tea down and sorted through his luggage for his laptop. Time to search for the latest goings on in the Balkans and see if he might find a clue to the truth.

Sucker.

Weigel was holding back, and Raven wanted to know why. If his wife was a pawn in a bigger scheme Weigel didn't want to admit, perhaps a victim of illegal dealings in which her husband engaged, he wanted to get her out of harm's way. He'd deal with Weigel's end of the matter after.

Raven figured he might pick up more pieces of the puzzle when he met with Erika the next afternoon. He'd play dumb for a while, maintain the sense of urgency, and see what developed.

PHILIP WEIGEL HATED traveling without his usual extravagance. Erika's BMW 740Li was nice but nowhere near the Bentley he usually drove. But he had to stay off the radar; he knew his home, and mostly likely the Bentley, was bugged.

Defying Oliver Kohlberg had come with a risk, and he was only now beginning to understand the risk.

But he had no desire to reverse his decision.

He rode shotgun as Erika drove onto the freeway. His bodyguard sat in the back.

Erika said, "Trying to fool Raven is a big mistake. We *need* to tell him."

Weigel clenched his left fist. He didn't need her on his neck. But she also wasn't wrong. He loosened his fingers and replied, "Erika, trust me. If we don't keep him in the dark, he'll—"

"What?"

"Kill us all."

"Your friend probably has that in mind as a backup plan. Tell Raven everything. Hand over Kohlberg on a plate."

"Just *drive*, Erika. Drive and don't talk. I don't feel like *talking* anymore."

Weigel sat still and felt hot. Everything he and Leslie had built was at risk. He never should have agreed to join Kohlberg's club. *The Fraternity.* A bunch of old men with delusions of running the world—what had he been thinking? He had never disagreed with Kohlberg's basic philosophy, but wholesale murder was too much to bear. Backing out didn't absolve him from responsibility, though. He'd done his part for "the plan" before his conscience took over and reminded him of who he was. He preferred to think the non-violent pacifist attitude of his youth influenced his change of mind, but the reality was "the plan" scared him shitless. He had trouble remembering his youth, after all, and the attitudes he'd carried then. What he did recall were only flashes of memory, the usual regrets and what-ifs; he had spent all his time focused on goals and never enjoyed the individual moments, or took the time to smell the roses his wife loved so much. And now she might be taken from him. Kohlberg wasn't messing around. Weigel was putting all the chips on Sam Raven to pull his head out of the fire.

His hopes and dreams depended on the success of Sam Raven.

And when Raven learned the truth?

Weigel had always been confident in his decisions; it was how he'd built his fortune, grew his investment empire. But Leslie's capture exposed the doubts behind the bravado.

He was glad to have Erika as an advisor. Her level head worked wonders while his mind spun out of control.

He glanced at the woman beside him. Her eyes were fixed on the road, her face tight with anger. He faced forward again.

They drove on in silence.

THE NEXT MORNING, Raven ate breakfast in the hotel restaurant. He sat near the windows in a back corner with a view of the pool. Nobody swam or occupied the loungers yet, but the forecast called for a hot day. If he came back at noon, he'd find the pool swarmed.

Dining room chatter muted his thoughts as he ate and re-read an email from Oscar Morey outlining the career of Philip Weigel.

The man started a recycling business in his 20s, catching the "green wave" from the late '90s through the early 2000s. Wise investments in tech and durable goods grew his fortune, and he'd left the recycling biz behind to become an angel investor to small companies perusing a green agenda. Various ups and downs multiplied and reduced his fortune over the years, but he stayed afloat investing in not-so-green companies as well. Raven noticed no defense involvement. He never backed R&D for new weapons, unlike many investors he knew of who liked profits generated by the mili-tary-government-industrial complex.

Weigel's personal background matched his business atti-tude. Dedicated pacifist. College activist. Usual do-gooder activity. Nothing in his background suggested anything nefarious. But something, a small detail, hadn't made the official biography. Amidst the charitable foundation and promotion of "good causes", Oscar had discovered nothing to suggest why somebody wanted to kidnap Weigel's wife.

Raven chewed a slice of bacon and thought.

Even the best had weak moments, and Philip Weigel was no exception, but what had he done?

Raven clicked on the attachments Oscar included with the email. Pictures of Weigel and his wife; more ribbon cuttings with only Leslie present; none of the photos stirred curiosity or interest until Raven clicked on the final picture.

The photograph showed Weigel in an animated conversa-tion with one Oliver Kohlberg.

Raven frowned. Had he found a clue?

Kohlberg was a controversial figure. On the outside, another billionaire investor with a strong interest in world affairs. Beneath the surface, rumors of subversion and skullduggery to force the tide of world events in directions he preferred. And those directions had zero to do with individual freedom or national sovereignty. Kohlberg allegedly wanted a single group of elites to control the world, with his chosen puppets at the helm.

Raven shook his head. The two possessed dramatically opposite points of view. Kohlberg invested in everything Weigel didn't like. The picture wasn't enough of a connection. Rich people met other rich people and the chat captured in the photograph might have been nothing more than a first and last meeting as they passed each other.

He'd find the truth another way, *after* pulling Leslie Weigel out of the line of fire.

Raven finished breakfast and returned to his room. Only a few hours until he had to meet Erika, and he had three phone calls to make.

He needed his Raiders for this one, the three hard-charging warriors he depended on when four heads were better than one.

They were:

Zaven "Darbo" Darbinian, an Armenian mercenary with tremendous experience in the world's regional wars.

Lia Kenisova, a Russia covert specialist, freelancer, as deadly as she was stunning.

Roger Justice, American mercenary, with an appropriate surname. Like Raven, he sought jobs where the underdog faced overwhelming odds, and fought to turn the tide. Like Raven, he didn't always accomplish the goal. But he never stopped trying.

All three were solid and reliable fighters who may have been for hire, but never for sale. He took out his phone and started dialing.

6

SOMEWHERE IN MARSEILLE

ROGER JUSTICE HAD BEEN IN FRANCE FOR A WEEK ON A RESCUE
job of his own, this one involving two young girls.

And he was almost out of time.

Roger rose from high brush, clutching a submachine gun
tight to his shoulder, the muzzle probing the dark night as he
rotated through a danger scan. The night-vision goggles over
his eyes bathed the area in a greenish glow, but he saw what
he needed to see. The farmhouse about forty yards ahead,
and two sentries walking a pattern around the structure.

The sentries, with slung automatic weapons, stayed about
twenty yards from the farmhouse. Their patrol covered
different sections of the property, but didn't extend into the
high grass beyond.

Roger Justice started forward in a crouch. The tall grass,
bleached from heat and dry weather, swished as he moved
over the uneven dirt beneath him. The sentries wouldn't
notice at this distance. Closer, maybe. But by then, they'd be
lined up in the Aimpoint infrared sights of Roger's .45 ACP

Kriss Vector SMG; he'd cancel whatever response they might have with the smack of hollow-point slugs.

The farmhouse sat smack in the middle of the field off outside the city, but not so far those inside had a long drive to the Port of Marseille. The farm had long gone dormant, the ground reclaimed by nature and overgrown, but the current owners kept up the house because they wanted seclusion and privacy.

Telephone towers sprouted out of the field like a row of toy soldiers, the hum of the lines almost audible if Roger stayed in place long enough. As he continued his advance, his breathing steady, the Vector's muzzle taking the lead, he heard nothing but the pulse in his own head, thought of nothing except his strike plan.

Roger wasn't working on his own. A global organization of former Navy SEALs and retired police officers carried out the search for the two girls; this particular case required a hitter with Roger's up-to-date abilities. A backup team waited with transport to get the girls away.

The group's intelligence on the farmhouse gang indicated this was merely a halfway stop before taking the girls to the port where they'd be shipped to a trafficking syndicate in Asia. Roger had to move fast. The time for surveillance had ended; now they needed to act, and he was the tip of the spear.

If the girls left France, they'd never be seen again.

Roger had a personal stake in the mission. His sister had been the victim of a kidnapping, snatched on her way home from school, on a day branded into his brain. He had no evidence of where she wound up or what happened, but after what he'd learned over the years of the fate of other kidnap victims, it almost didn't matter. She'd vanished one way or the other. And now he was making similar perps pay, delivering the kind of punishment they deserved.

The girls were sisters who had been riding their bikes near home when the kidnappers grabbed them off the street.

He halted his advance to take a knee, using the Vector's barrel to part the grass and look at the sentries.

Only two?

Roger frowned. Why the skeleton crew? They might have more inside, or, better for him, they were a gang so used to never facing an opposing force they didn't bother to put serious defenses in place. It was as if the guards were there to keep the girls *in* rather than keep somebody like Roger *out*.

He waited. He watched. A breeze rustled the tall grass.

Roger cut left.

The Port of Marseille, the girls' destination if Roger failed, had a lot of nooks and crannies used by human traffickers to spirit their cargo out to sea, unseen and unnoticed in the chaotic activity throughout the port. The port had earned the reputation as a hub of human trafficking over the last two decades, a proverbial 800-pound gorilla with law enforcement handcuffed by procedure and the need for evidence and warrants, and kept away with payoffs and corruption.

Roger completed his circle, well away from the 20-yard sentry, who was turning toward the direction of the highway. He picked up speed. The farmhouse sat in a circular clearing, a tall tree with the thickest trunk Roger had ever seen between the edge of the grass and the rear porch.

The greenish glow through the goggles was as familiar as a pocket comb to Roger, and he moved over the terrain with ease. Dropping prone short of the clearing, he once again scanned the immediate area. He was rigged for war and a fast getaway.

Along with the compact Kriss Vector .45 ACP submachine gun, he carried a smoke grenade and a flash-bang stun grenade on his utility belt. Extra magazines rode in pouches on his combat vest, with a .45-caliber sidearm strapped to his right hip. He'd had a gunsmith tune the HK USP to his own specifications.

For the ride out of the hell zone, he had two of the former SEALs waiting at the edge of the road 100 yards away with a souped-up four-door capable of outrunning anything the opposition might employ for pursuit. If any survived.

Roger waited while the sentries completed their circle of the house. They didn't pass behind him. They'd scan the rear from the side of the farmhouse, and then continued their circuit around front. There was nothing behind Roger but more grass, rolling hills, and telephone towers. They didn't think they'd face an attack from the rear. Well, he'd teach them never to make such a mistake again. Too bad they wouldn't live to apply the lesson.

Roger pulled a flash-bang grenade from his belt and tugged out the pin. He waited for the sentries to turn back his way once more.

The door on the back porch opened, a wide blast of interior light landing on Roger as he prepared his toss. He winced as the night vision goggles amplified the light, quickly sweeping his left hand up, knocking the goggles away, but his bare eyes needed time to adjust.

"Hey!"

Roger looked. The big tree partially blocked his view, but the man emerging from the porch made himself clear with the light behind him. He dropped a cigarette and lighter and pawed for a pistol on his hip. Roger threw the flash-bang on instinct. It landed square in the middle of the man's chest and detonated, the man's piercing scream filling the night along with the feverish blast of bright light and a boom.

Roger snatched up the Vector as the sentries converged, his eyes now adjusted, the closer of the two guards firing his weapon. Roger rolled as rounds chewed the ground. He came up in front of the tree, easing back the Vector's trigger. His own .45-cal salvo smacked into the sentry, stitching him from abdomen to neck. He fell back, only to reveal his partner, who was angling for his own shot. He never fired. A follow-up Vector burst cut him down.

The man at the porch had fallen to the ground. He screamed and struggled to rise. Roger found him with a hole in his shirt, the skin underneath blackened, a portion of his face also horribly burned. Roger kicked the man's gun away and left him there, charging into the house, sweeping the Vector left and right, as he searched every room in the house.

The empty house.

Where are they?

His pulse quickened. He saw evidence of occupation, judging by the amount of trash, and he found wall-mounted restraints in one of the rooms; along with a girl's tennis shoe in the middle of the floor.

Was he too late?

No! Can't be...

If all he'd done was kill a few lackeys, the mission was a total failure. But there was no time to think about failed intelligence. He needed information *now* and he knew who to ask.

The groans of the man on the porch once again reached his ears. Roger landed hard on the man, jamming a knee between his legs as he leaned over and looked into the man's agonized face.

"Where are the girls?"

The man moaned. Roger slapped him hard and repeated the question, adding: "Tell me and I'll get you a medic."

The man instead tried to spit and shove Roger off of him, but Roger grabbed one of the man's hands, twisting, and pulled back the man's pinky finger until bone snapped.

The man screamed again.

"Where are the girls?"

The man, panting, tried to slow his breathing. Tears streamed down his face. Finally, he pushed out some words.

"Beneath…the house. Back room. Trap door under carpet."

Roger left him in agony, slinging the Vector as he dashed back inside. He found the room in the back of the house, the master bedroom, and turned on the lights. He had to get on his hands and knees to find the cut in the carpet, but once he peeled back the sliced portion, he saw the trap door. The door was solid steel, hinged to the hardwood beneath the carpet. Roger flicked the latches, grabbed an attached steel ring, and raised the lid.

Gasping. Crying. The sounds of two frightened girls trapped in a pit of darkness.

But they were alive.

He'd found them.

Roger called his backup crew. They arrived in the souped-up four-door but Roger made them wait a minute before he climbed into the car, too.

He went back and shot the man on the porch.

———————

ROGER SHUT the door to his hotel and tossed the overcoat and heavy kit bag in the closet. He had half his clothes off with his mind on a shower when his cell chimed. He answered.

"It's Sam."

"Hey."

"You sound tired."

"Just finished a job."

"I got another for you if you want to come to the US."

"Where?"

"Florida," Raven said. "Rescue job."

"I just finished a rescue."

"Success?"

"I'm pleased, yes." Roger smiled at his reflection in the bathroom mirror.

"I'll send the details then. Usual fee."

"I'll be on a plane in the morning."

7

SOMEWHERE IN ARMENIA

HE WENT BY THE NAME DARBO, BUT THE CHOPPED VERSION OF his surname was the only thing short about Zaven Darbinian.

Which meant the jerk taking a shot at him had to aim high. Mistake—he aimed *too* high and the bullet parted Darbo's hair. But he felt the burn of the passing bullet. It whined off the wall behind him.

"Nice try!" Darbo shouted. He raised a pistol and fired twice in return, but he had a further disadvantage: no target. He fired for effect to make the sniper on the roof across the street run for cover. If he exposed himself in the process, even better. But he didn't.

And then rushing footsteps told Darbo the sniper wasn't alone, and he began thinking it might be a good idea to vacate himself.

He'd never should have agreed to the job.

Job? Hell, he was doing a favor for his cousin. He was working for *free*!

But he wasn't supposed to end up dead in the process.

He was in Yerevan, Armenia, responding to his cousin's SOS. Cousin Emin had a problem with his brother Varos losing his temper and overturning tables at a bar. The bar's owner had objected to the way Varos was treating women in his establishment, and kindly asked him to stop. Varos, tanked, and trying to save face in front of the two thugs he hung out with, let the bar owner know he disagreed with the request by overturning tables and breaking stuff and making what should have been a fun night into a serious problem involving the police.

And Darbo's cousins were the type of people who wanted nothing, zero, zip, *nada*, to do with the police.

Varos created a powder-keg situation and it was up to Darbo to pour water on the fuse.

Cousin Emin was a big shot Armenian mobster; he controlled vice in a large portion of the city. The bar owner, Matsag Sarian, was equally powerful in a rival syndicate. He'd be within his rights to hurt Emin's business as Varos had hurt the bar's. A quick summit led Emin and Matsag to a solution. Emin promised to pay for the damage, and add 10% to the bill for Matsag's time and trouble. In exchange for not going after Varos, Emin also promised to deal with his little brother personally and rotate him to another location where he wouldn't bother anybody.

Matsag Sarian agreed.

Emin asked Darbo to deliver the money. Darbo said okay. Easy gig, he was able to visit old friends, have a little "home week" action; Darbo saw no reason to charge Emin since his cousin was taking care of his hotel, food, and travel. But now somebody was shooting at him, and the shooter had no idea how to fire a gun from a rooftop.

It was four a.m. but there was plenty of light. Nobody needed the sun when streetlamps lit the road and bars and restaurants left some of the window neon shining despite being closed.

Darbo parked curbside and crossed the sidewalk toward an alley. He'd been told to use the bar's side entrance. Before he reached the alley, he felt the shot pass overhead, the crack of the report, and then running feet.

As Darbo whirled and pull his SIG-Sauer P-226 9 mm, he looked across the opposite side of the street, and on the roof of the three-story clothing store. The sniper who couldn't hit what he aimed at finally showed himself. He ran to the far edge of the roof, out of Darbo's sight, and the fleeting glimpse of the figure's outline made ID impossible. Darbo had a feeling he knew who the man was, or at least who had sent him.

He pivoted left at the sound of the rushing footsteps. He grasped the P-226 in his right hand, and the wrapped parcel of money in his left. He wanted to drop the parcel, but it was probably the objective of the men attacking him.

He fired twice with the SIG extended, then ran to the front end of his car. It was lousy cover. He had two incoming and a third working his way down from the roof. Darbo had no doubt the wanna-be sniper was coming to join the fight.

Darbo's first two 9 mm sizzlers at least helped. Both slugs puckered the chest of one goon running to him, the fellow collapsing in a clumsy tumble, his head cracking against the concrete. A gun fell out of the waistband of his jeans.

The second stopped short. He and Darbo made eye contact. The second punk was young, early 20s, and made a squeaking noise as he raised the pistol in his hand. Unlike his partner, he'd been smart enough to draw before the rush.

But sudden movement on his right made Darbo hesitate. The "sniper" rounded the corner across the street and ran at him. He still carried his rifle.

Darbo dived left. The young punk fired and missed.

Darbo's return fire was all over the place, too—over the punk's head, past a shoulder, even straight between his knees as Darbo landed with a grunt on the sidewalk. He kept the parcel clutched close to his body; he landed like a football player inches from the end zone with the ball pinned beneath as the entire team piled on top. In other words, *ouch!* He felt bent in half as his body rested half on, and half off, the parcel.

But the kid wasn't *all* dumb. He turned to run. Darbo wasn't *all* hurt and miserable, and he knew better than to let an enemy get away. He steadied his aim and fired twice. He hit the punk in the back, both shots scoring, the young punk arching his back as he began to fall face first. Darbo didn't take the time to watch the kid hit the ground. He had the so-called sniper to deal with.

"I want the money, Darbo!"

The Armenian mercenary hadn't been wrong. The sniper was Emin's brother, Varos; the goons had been his buddies, and he was really making a simple gig a pain in the neck.

Darbo rolled onto his back with the SIG ready. *Sorry, cuz,* he thought.

Varos appeared over the hood of Darbo's car with his rifle tucked into his shoulder and the muzzle zeroed on Darbo's face. Darbo fired first. Varos's body stiffened as the 9 mm slug drilled through his left shoulder. Varos screamed and fell over. Darbo ran over to him, jerked the rifle from his grasp, and swung the SIG against his head. Varos passed out. Darbo dragged him onto the sidewalk so he could get his car out later.

The Armenian merc felt eyes on him as he set Varos on the sidewalk, eyes hidden behind the bar's front façade. He hurried down the alley to the side door, and knocked using the butt of his gun. Then he put the gun away. Matsag himself opened the door and frowned.

"Is there a problem?" the bar owner said.

"You ain't kiddin'. You're gonna have cops all over here in two minutes…" and he explained the shooting.

"Get inside. We saw most of it."

Matsag stepped back. Darbo entered and passed the parcel to the other man.

"Here. This is yours. Count the money. I'll sit and be quiet."

Matsag examined the parcel. In the low light inside, it was hard to tell the look on his face. A woman stood behind the bar watching them both. Matsag told her to pour whatever Darbo wanted while he counted the money. Darbo asked for two shots of Makers Mark. Matsag walked out of sight. Darbo turned to the woman.

"Come here often?"

She placed the two shot glasses before him. "Every night."

Darbo downed the shots and heard sirens in the distance.

"Maybe pour me a double next," he told her.

The lady delivered his drink and he offered her a silent salute before taking a swallow. His phone rang. Darbo fished the cell out of a pocket and answered.

"Darbo?"

"Yeah."

"It's Sam."

"What's going on?"

"You working? I need shooters."

"You paying?"

"Yeah."

"Where you at?"

"Florida. Rescue job. Usual fee."

"Text me the details and I'll be on the first plane out once the sun comes up."

"Will do. See you soon."

Darbo ended the call and smiled at the lady behind the bar. "I didn't get your name."

"You can call me the boss's wife."

Darbo blanched. "Oh."

8

SOMEWHERE IN MOSCOW

HER NAME WAS LIA KENISOVA, AND SHE DIDN'T GO AFTER small fish.

As a former member of the GRU, Russian military intelligence, she maintained a wide variety of connections in her career as a freelancer. One such connection, a former colleague, now worked for a Russian firm dealing with software and high-tech business products. Somebody was selling their development information and leaking intellectual property secrets to rivals. Her former colleague suggested to his boss they bring her in to deal with their main suspect and see if he was indeed guilty; for Lia, the job was a bit boring, but she didn't mind doing a favor for a friend—of course, she wasn't working free. Her client paid her usual asking price.

Lia's work normally covered retrieving stolen property for the wealthy, counter-terrorist missions when the Motherland was threatened, and other nefarious activities—her old boss had nicknamed her "Piranha". Whatever she sank her teeth into, she destroyed.

She entered *Night Flight*, one of the best clubs in Moscow, where the elite wined and dined. Or was that *whine* and dine? She couldn't keep track. It was the place to hang out if you passed the bruiser of a bouncer at the front door. All Lia had to do was smile, mention her former colleague's name, and slip under the barrier once the bouncer lifted the velvet rope. A chorus of hoots from those still in line assaulted her ears, but Lia knew what they didn't. The bouncer was also ex-GRU. Lia's client had slipped him something extra to allow her access without delay.

Lia was dressed to kill. Slinky black dress, red lipstick, heels. The strapless top pressed her breasts together to create the perfect valley for a schmuck to get lost in should his eyes drift there. The diamond pendant around her neck promised a few glances, for sure, and would lead those same eyes to her tits. The chain around her neck was like the yellow brick road. She needed her target enthralled, sucked in, locked into a bear trap from which he had no way to escape.

She was currently a blonde. She'd been a redhead for the last few years, since there were so few redheads in Russia. The contrast between her blonde hair and black dress was another eye-catching ploy. And she'd let her hair grow so the curled locks stretched down her back and tickled her slender neck.

Electronic dance music thump-bumped as she moved through the crowd, their dancing matching the beat of the so-called music, which Lia despised. The hot temperature inside was a welcome change from the chill of the Moscow night. She hadn't brought a coat or wrap. Baby had to show off the curves.

Those not dancing crowded tables, pressed elbow-to-elbow without any hint of privacy. You didn't come to *Night Flight* to have dinner by candle light. The low light and strobe flashes from the dance floor had a way of taking you out of reality, but Lia wasn't about to let down her guard. She had a job to do. She needed to earn her substantial paycheck.

Her target sat at the bar and looked haggard, as if he was on his sixth vodka tonic and tenth strike out of the evening.

Peter Kryukov was only a little taller than Lia. He was blonde, too, with a square jaw, and a decent physique for somebody who worked in an office all day. Another couple sat next to him; on his right sat two women. Maybe they were whores. If they were, neither was doing a good job, because they should have been all over Kryukov. She was about to elbow the bitches out of the way when the women closed the deal with a porky dude she hadn't noticed and the trio walked away.

Lia took the stool vacated by one of the women, close to Kryukov, and ordered a martini. The music wasn't so loud in the bar, but she still felt the floor vibrating through the legs of the barstool. *Thump-bump-bump.*

The bartender brought her martini and she took the glass by the bowl, sipping the icy beverage. She examined her long, sharp fingernails. She'd painted them red. Because *duh* she was Russian.

"Your nails look like apples."

Lia turned her head slowly to raise an eyebrow at Kryukov's awkward opening line. He slurred most of the words.

"Can I suck on them to keep the doctor away?"

He laughed.

Lia didn't fight her smile. He'd done half of her job for her, and she had him on the hook.

"Worst line I have ever heard," she said. She sipped her drink.

"Do you hear a lot of them?"

"Men usually don't talk until I let them."

"Oh, so you like being in control? Want to tie me up?"

"I think you need a different type of girl," Lia said. She started to slide off the stool but he grabbed her arm. She snapped her head around and let him see her meanest glare.

"Please. I'm sorry. It's been a long day. I didn't mean to offend."

Lia shook her head. Men apologized too much. Used to be you could count on Russian men to double down and exercise dominance. No more. Too much American influence. If she didn't find a traditional Russian man, she'd stay single forever.

She held Kryukov's gaze a moment and almost detected a pleading look in his eye. Good grief, he was a thirsty fish, all right.

"All right, another chance."

He smiled, showing his teeth. It was a nice smile. Shame what might happen to it before the night ended.

Unless he cooperated.

She finished her martini and he ordered her another and told the bartender to put the first one on his tab, too. Then they started a normal conversation. Kryukov told her about his job with her former colleague's company, but he was smart enough not to mention any thefts he might be involved with. He didn't ask about her work. She had a cover story ready, but he was already playing into her hand, and all she had to do was reel in the catch.

Which she did, after a third martini and whatever umpteenth vodka tonic he swallowed. He handled his liquor well. Talking to her actually seemed to sharpen him. He only slurred a few words, and he managed to walk straight after she suggested they leave the noisy club. And go somewhere private.

He had a company car and called the driver with his cell. They waited at the curb for ten minutes, the line outside having grown longer since Lia arrived. The bouncer refused to let anybody inside. Lia didn't make eye contact with the bouncer. If she ever saw him again during a job, she wouldn't remember his face anyway.

She told Kryukov to give the driver her apartment address. He didn't do as much talking during the drive as he had in the club. He'd switched from chatterbox to quiet.

To get his attention again, she put a hand on his leg and slowly moved it across the fabric of his slacks to his crotch. She squeezed.

He grunted, shifted, but didn't respond. Great. He was trying to play cool. Hard to get. What was he, seventeen?

She withdrew her hand and decided to wait until he figured out whatever he was planning to do. *Her* plan was already well in motion. All she needed was him, in her apartment, with a drink in his hand.

The driver made a final turn, went one more block, and pulled over in front of her building. With a smile, she beckoned him to follow her out of the car. He didn't need any further encouragement.

The glass walls of Lia's apartment overlooked the bright lights of the city. It wasn't hers, of course. Her former colleague had set it up. She only had the place for the night.

Kryukov put his hands on his hips and admired the view while she mixed drinks. He started idle chit-chat about how long she'd lived there, and she glanced over her shoulder to make sure his attention was on the city lights. She palmed a vial from the back of her neck where she'd taped it. Her curly hair had concealed the vial. Cracking the cap open, Lia poured the clear contents into the vodka tonic.

She moved to the couch, positioned to face the glass wall and the view of Moscow, and clicked her tongue to get his attention. He smiled and crossed to her, taking his drink. They clinked glasses. She sipped her glass while he took a long drink of his.

Perfect.

"Sit down."

He placed the vodka on the table in front of the couch and sat. She stood in front of him and bit her lower lip as he regarded her with eager eyes.

"Want to reach up my dress?"

"Sure."

"Move your right hand."

Kryukov blinked as he made the effort. His hand did not move.

"Um."

"Move your left leg."

"I can't!"

Panic.

Lia sat on the table, crossed her legs, and pressed her lips together. "Well, isn't that interesting. But there's a reason."

"Uh."

"I've poisoned you. I will only give you the antidote if you answer my questions."

"What?"

"As you can see, you can still talk, but the rest of your body is paralyzed."

He strained to move any part of his body; failed. He began to sweat.

"You told me who you work for, but what you didn't tell me was if you're stealing secrets from your company and selling them to the highest bidder. Yes?"

Kryukov tried to nod; couldn't. He said, "Yes!" More panic now. Sweat dripped down the side of his face.

"The poison will take twenty-four hours to kill you, by the way."

Kryukov let out a high-pitched squeal. Lia laughed.

"Who do you pass the information to?"

Kryukov hurriedly explained the entire scheme. He was

selling data to a man named Dusa Gusin. Lia knew all about the Bill Gates of Moscow, which is how he presented himself —rich, powerful, a force to reckon with. The truth was Gusin was broke. He'd made several bad calls with products he couldn't sell, and his competitors overtook him. Kryukov took the stolen data and passed it to Gusin's daughter, Misha, who didn't work for her father but instead owned and operated a boutique shop where Kryukov left dead drops for her father to collect. Lia didn't bother to make notes. She had a recorder in her purse taking down every word he said.

When he finished, she said, "If I give you the antidote, what are you going to do?"

"Go home!"

"And?"

"Never tell anybody about this!"

"And?"

"Um."

"You're going to tell your boss what you have done, correct?"

"Yes!"

Lia reached behind her neck for a second taped vial. She broke the cap and leaned over Kryukov, forcing his mouth open. She poured the liquid onto his tongue and pushed his mouth closed. Kryukov swallowed.

Lia sat on the table again. "There. Wasn't so hard, right?"

Kryukov began testing his fingers and toes and arms and legs as the antidote took effect. Everything moved on command.

Lia said, "I recorded our chat, so don't try and back out."

Kryukov looked at her. His face remained blank at first, but then a flare of anger took over. He lunged, but Lia had expected the move. An elbow strike to the temple toppled Kryukov. He fell onto the carpet between the couch and table.

She stepped over him and gathered her things. She'd deliver the recording to her client and let him sort out what to do next. For her, it was mission accomplished and onto the next.

———

LIA DIDN'T LIVE in Moscow any longer. When she left, she meant to stay away. But the client had provided a nice hotel. She returned to the building and carried her heels across the lobby, ignoring the feel of the lobby tile on her nyloned feet. Back in her room, she dropped the shoes in the closet and stripped off her dress.

Thirty minutes under hot water washed away the night, and she exited with a bathrobe and towel wrapped around her head. Sitting on the bed, she stared at the wall. She was worn out, felt numb, and only wanted to sleep. Swallowing a sleeping pill with a glass of water, she then turned down the bed and started to untie the robe when her cell rang.

She answered. "Yes?"

"Lia. It's Sam."

"I'm tired. What do you want?"

Raven laughed on the other end of the line. "I got a job and I need shooters. Interested?"

"What's happening?"

"Rescue. Usual fee."

"I want raise. Ten percent more."

"No. We're on a budget. It's deliver or nothing. You in or out?"

"Fine. Cheap American trash. I'll be there."

"Russian bitch. I'll send you the details."

Lia cracked a smile. "See you soon, darling," she said.

She turned off the lights and climbed into bed.

9

With his Raiders on the way, Raven drove to Erika's hotel for their noon appointment and more details on the mission.

Oscar hadn't had any luck tracing Erika's background, but Raven wasn't surprised. His buddy wasn't a miracle worker. Raven had no last name, no picture; for now, she was a dead end, but worth trying. Raven looked forward to trying to get her to reveal more about herself.

He found her hotel on the beach overlooking the ocean. He paused before entering, letting his mind wander as he watched the blue waves crash on shore. The breeze carried a salt-tinged mist, and the wind ruffled his hair. The ocean always calmed him. The rhythm of the waves soothed his anxious spirit more than any woman or alcohol might; he'd never failed to reset after a period of ocean exposure. Maybe he needed rest more than a job where the client wasn't telling the whole truth. He could walk away, call off Darbo and Roger and Lia, and find a private cottage on the beach. Forget everything and everybody until his mind settled once again.

Just go.

He touched the locket hanging beneath his shirt. The locket he never opened. The locket containing the ghosts who urged him on.

You can't.

Why?

Because...

Leslie Weigel. The victim. Her husband might have secrets, he might have entered into shady dealings which put his wife at risk, but why should she suffer for his sins?

She's not as innocent as you think.

You won't know until you bring her back.

There was no sense in fighting. His path had been chosen for him, and he knew, deep down, he couldn't turn away even if he wanted to. Raven turned from the ocean, stowed his melancholy, and entered the hotel.

ERIKA ANSWERED HIS KNOCK. She smiled; he frowned. She'd cut her hair, replacing the long flowing mane with a short high-and-tight.

"Come in," she said.

Raven entered. A laptop and map sat on the desk against the forward wall. The bed had been hastily made; the comforter only pulled up over the pillows. She shut the door and flipped the lock.

"We can have lunch sent up if you want." She walked by him to the desk but didn't sit. She wore frayed blue jeans and a loose T-shirt, but the haircut held his attention.

"Why the chop top?" Raven said.

"Can't have long hair if you're going into combat."

"Who's going into combat?"

"I am."

"Not with my crew. I don't know you. Neither do they. I'm bringing real cutthroats with me. This job is fishy enough without variables tagging along."

She folded her arms and looked mad. "Well, tough shit, Mr. Raven. Me and another operator selected by Mr. Weigel *will* be joining your crew."

"Then why do you need me? If you have the capability—"

"We need an experienced leader and that's not my area of expertise."

"What *is* your area of expertise, Erika?"

She gestured to the laptop and map on the desk. "I know where to look, because I knew what to look *for*. I can run, jump and shoot, but I've never led a small unit. *Any* unit, for that matter."

"You're a follower."

"My strengths are elsewhere. As well as invaluable. You wouldn't have any idea where to start without me."

"Where did you learn these skills?"

"Where do you *think*? CIA, SIS, Mossad—I got around before going into business for myself."

"I'm curious what your business is."

"Private intelligence. Security. Valuable contacts."

"Why does Philip Weigel need a private spy?"

"I'm not *spying* on anybody. I provide Weigel's security— his offices, *and* his computer systems."

"And you're a commando, too. Quite a bonus."

"Extra cost option."

Raven smiled without humor. He wanted to ask if she'd found the bugs Weigel feared, but the antagonism between them was about to burst. He wasn't trying to be petty. He didn't appreciate the kind of surprise she was dropping on him, and he knew the Raiders would object at a much higher volume. "Don't expect a warm welcome."

"But you'll vouch for me."

"Sure."

"Say it like you mean it."

Raven shook his head. "Let's see what I think *after* you show me how good you are."

"Take a seat, Mr. Raven."

She turned quick but Raven caught the flash of anger across her face. She dropped into the chair in front of the desk while Raven set up a folding chair and joined her. She orientated the map so he had a better view, and hit two keys on the computer with more force than necessary.

Raven wondered if he was letting his doubts dictate his attitude.

Focus on the rescue. We'll sort out the rest after.

RAVEN STUDIED the map while Erika prepared the laptop. The map showed northern Serbia, with three circles in a large forest area.

"We have three possible locations," Erika said, "and we'll need to check out each one to see where the kidnappers have stashed Leslie Weigel."

"Why did they take her all the way to Serbia?" Raven said.

The implications weren't good, Raven knew. There was only one organization big enough, strong enough, and crazy enough to undertake pulling off a kidnapping in the US. The Serbian Mafia. Tough nuts, all of them. Smuggling, arms trafficking, *human* trafficking, drugs; they had fingers deep in those pies and much more. If they weren't directly involved, they had allowed another crew to work in their territory, which meant big money had changed hands. Whoever Weigel had pissed off wasn't fooling around. Raven figured if Weigel didn't come across with the truth, and the team failed, poor Leslie might find herself on a ship to a sex slave auction, or worse. At her age they might simply cut her throat and call it a day, unless they found a Saudi prince who liked older women. Raven shifted in his seat.

"I don't know," Erika answered, pulling Raven out of his thoughts. "But my best sources say it's one of these three areas."

"Are these camps or what?"

"I'm not sure. What I *don't* have is satellite capability."

"It's risky," Raven said. "Best way to check might be a drone, with a camera, we fly it over each and see what we find. Otherwise, we risk engaging with enemies not related to the objective, and we won't be able to spare the ammo or the bodies."

"I'll get whatever equipment you need."

"What's on the computer?"

"The best pictures I could find of the region so we at least know the terrain," she said. Erika rotated the screen to Raven. He watched as she clicked through the pictures. Forest. A lot of green. Tough-looking mountains and wilderness. Streams and lakes. But another thought leapt out at him.

"We have to watch the terrain, any bandits working the area, and wherever we find Mrs. Weigel. Tell me some good news."

"We'll have air transport in and out," she said. "When do your people get here?"

"They're on the way. Probably tonight."

"Philip will want to meet everybody, and it will take the rest of the day to get the transport finalized."

"What's the real story, Erika?"

"What do you mean?"

"Why do you call him *Philip*?"

"It's not what you think."

Raven bit his tongue and turned his attention to the map

once more, cycles through the computer pictures again, and considered the computer images useless. They told him nothing of the objective or what else they might face; all he knew was they needed good hiking gear along with the rest of their combat equipment.

Which brought to mind another question.

"Weapons and gear. Squared away?"

"I'll show you the shopping list," Erika said. She opened a document and showed Raven the list of ordered items.

Six Heckler & Koch 416 carbines in 5.56mm with ammunition and eight spare magazines for each. Grenades—smoke, high-explosive, buckshot. Two HK320 grenade launchers with assorted shells. Night vision units, body armor, com units. The list also included a supply of MREs and medical kits.

"Impressive," Raven said. "Ammo for our pistols?"

"We have .45 and 9 mm, don't worry."

"How did you know there'd be six?"

"You always call the same people for help, Mr. Raven."

Another detectible pattern.

Raven grinned. He had no idea who Erika was, where she came from, or her last name, but he had to admit she was growing on him.

"Call me Sam," he told her. "I'm beginning to think I should change my earlier point of view."

"Don't change on my account." She smiled.

GO SAVE ON MY GRAVE... W

Once more, Cato, though the computer pictures spun, and
connected the controller to the gesture. They told him
nothing of the objective or what else they might face, all he
knew is they needed good things you along with the rest
of their daily equipment.

With breakable to reasonable situation

Overcome and sit at Surrenders...

"I'll show you the shopping file" Index of Net grabbed a
document and showed her in the list of current items.

Very Used to a Rich in explaine...a bottom and simon,
button and ghost state—long style. two each Order to a
smokeless sub-explosive buckshot. Two '84,320 remake
table box with assorted shelf. Night vision thing, body
memorie compliance. The list also included a supply of ...

10

RAVEN HAD A FINAL MEETING WITH PHILIP WEIGEL BEFORE THE
Raiders arrived. They had 72 hours before the ransom was
due, and Philip had assurances from the kidnappers his wife
would remain unharmed in the meantime. He was prepared
to send them the money via wire transfer if Raven and his
team couldn't reach her in time. Weigel didn't look at Raven
as he spoke, but into his glass of scotch instead; he didn't
appear to have been hitting the booze hard, but whatever
sapped his attention showed in the stress evident on his face.
Raven didn't want to push him harder until they had his wife
safely home. But he was tempted. He wanted the truth.

And not because he wanted to catch Weigel in a lie. If
there was more going on than met the eye, Raven might be
able to lend another hand, and solve the problem for good.
But he couldn't help if Weigel didn't trust him enough—yet.
Maybe when Leslie was home, he'd open up.

Seventy-two hours wasn't a lot of time when they faced a
12-hour flight across the ocean. Then there was the combat
they'd face. Too loud, too intense, and the Serbian government might show up to ask what was going on. Then they'd

face real trouble—Raven and his crew illegally in the country, armed to the teeth, and he didn't think Weigel had the pull to bail them out should they end up in a Serbian jail cell.

But where's the fun in no risk?

At least, that's what the Raiders thought of the matter.

Darbo arrived first, but Roger Justice and Lia Kenisova weren't far behind. Raven invited them to his hotel room for a briefing and introduction to the players involved, though neither Weigel, Erika, or anybody associated with them, including the sixth operator Erika wanted to bring, were present. Raven showed them the pictures and map, and shared Oscar's information. He asked Darbo if he knew the area they were going to, and Darbo had indeed been there on a previous job.

"It's where groups of Serbian mafia hide their stuff, people, gear, all that. But they're mixed with roving pirate crews who also use the area. There's a gentleman's agreement to not mess with each other's stuff or territory, and they managed to keep the peace, but any outsiders are fair game."

Raven asked if the mob would interfere with outsiders.

Darbo told him no. "It isn't in in the best interest of the mafia, but the pirates will mess with us for sure if they happen by."

Lia Kenisova quipped they might need more ammunition.

Roger promised to take care of the problems any pirates introduced as long as he could handle one of the HK320 grenade launchers. But he said it with a smile. Raven promised to issue him one of the two; he wasn't sure who'd get the other.

Lia asked about Erika. Raven gave her the rundown of his experience so far. He described her in detail, Darbo asking for more with a leer on his face, much to Lia's disgust; she called him an idiot. Darbo laughed. Roger observed with quiet interest. Raven shook his head. His Raiders never changed.

But Lia did think she knew who Erika was.

"Erika Kruger," the Russian woman said. "I think. Ran into her and a man named Anton Kruger on a job; he was ex-German intelligence, and they were married. They delivered the intel on my target. She wasn't a redhead, though."

"You were a redhead the last time I saw you," Raven said. "When you see Erika tomorrow, you can tell me for sure. She knows all about us, me specifically. Whoever she is, and whoever her contacts are, they are wired throughout the world. We haven't been keeping secrets from anybody."

Roger said, "Bother you?"

"A little."

"If she's friendly," Lia said, "who cares?"

"It's the what if she's not friendly question I'm bothered by," Raven said. "She's not coming along so much to help, but to make sure we don't find out what she and Weigel are hiding."

"You think?" Roger said.

"Positive."

"And if we do learn something?" Roger said.

"She and her friend might be there to keep us from bringing back any secrets."

"Let's be nice," Lia added, "but ready to kill them. Okay?"

"Couldn't have said it better," Raven told her.

The meeting continued another hour before disintegrating into general chit chat. The crew ordered dinner and caught up with their recent pasts and Raven eventually suggested they close up and get some rest. They'd meet the others tomorrow, and Raven didn't want anybody looking tired.

ERIKA FOUND Philip Weigel in his study, in a corner chair, holding a drink. He stared ahead at nothing in particular. The typical thousand-yard stare. The man had much on his mind, and Erika knew 90% of it because the same thoughts weighed down her shoulders, too.

"You've been drinking all day," she said. She sat near him in another chair and crossed her legs.

"I'm fine. I'm taking it slow."

"Is it helping?"

"Not at all."

"What are you thinking about?"

"I should have left Oliver when you first told me."

"Maybe I didn't tell you hard enough."

Weigel shook his head. "No, it's my fault. I wanted to instead believe he was right. The world needs change—"

"Not his kind."

"Let me finish. I don't want to argue. But, yes, I get it now. Especially—"

"Because we can't stop him? The plot's in motion?"

"I know we can beat him, but not alone. Do you think Raven will—"

"Right now, Raven only wants to get Mom back." She left the chair and moved behind him, taking away his glass and placing it on a side table. She leaned over to hug him around the neck; he grasped her hands in return.

"When we're done, we'll see about the rest," she said.

"Does he have any idea?"

"No. I kept my word. I haven't told him anything."

"You've been very brave, Erika."

"You worry enough for the two of us."

"If Anton were here—"

"He's not," she snapped. "We can wish a thousand time but it won't bring him back. It's *us*. And *maybe* Raven. Nobody else." She stood. "You need to go to bed, Dad. Big day tomorrow."

"Erika?"

"What?"

"Be careful. I can't lose both of you."

"You won't lose *either* of us," she said. "See you in the morning."

She left him in the study and went down the hall to the spare bedroom. The home her parents now lived in wasn't the one in which she'd grown up; she had no room of her own any longer. The guest room was generic in decoration but at least the bed was soft and the sun didn't blaze through the window in the morning.

She cleaned her teeth and climbed into bed, but what made her teary wasn't the thought of Kohlberg's goons holding her mother hostage. No, her father had to get drunk and mention Anton.

Her late husband would have brought in a mercenary army ten times bigger than what Raven mustered, and the Kohlberg goons would have never known what hit them.

But he was gone.

It was only her and her father and Raven's team, now.

They'd get her mother back, and she'd do Anton proud.

11

THEY WERE LATE.

Raven and his crew watched the pilots of Weigel's private jet do their exterior pre-flight checks. They waited in a corner of the hanger at the far end of the runway. At least the hangar was comfortable—Weigel had installed decent insulation, and included a sitting area with chairs and a coffee table, which included a pair of vending machines for coffee and sodas. Raven stood while his team sat, and he felt his impatience growing. They had their luggage ready to go, suitcases and packs containing their personal weapons and other necessities. Erika had promised they'd get a look at the weapons and equipment Weigel was providing before departure.

But Erika was late.

Had something happened? Raven didn't want to call Weigel and start a panic. He checked his watch. Fifteen minutes late. If he hadn't had so many doubts about Philip Weigel and the woman who kept her cards close to her chest, he might have felt better. Fifteen minutes wasn't terribly late.

But when you held no trust in the people you were working for, any unexplained delay only added to his discomfort.

"How long till you sound the alarm, Sam?" Roger Justice said. He sipped a Pepsi.

"I'll give her another ten minutes." Raven began to pace.

"Sit and relax," Lia said. "Don't pace like you're a prisoner."

"Easy for you to say."

The time limit bothered Raven the most. They had three places to check, other bad actors to potentially deal with, and not enough time—as far as he was concerned. They needed a little luck on this one, and he hoped Murphy was busy bothering somebody else so he and his team caught a break.

But he knew it was unlikely. This mission would go down to the wire. Weigel might have to pay the ransom while they were in-country, but it wasn't the solution Raven wanted. Ideally, they'd free Mrs. Weigel and get her home before the time limit forced her husband to make the sizeable bank transfer.

They'd create luck by dealing with expected problems, which were common to all missions, before they turned the effort into a disaster. It was the *unexpected* problems Raven knew they'd have to deal with on the fly.

It can never be easy, he thought.

Raven turned his attention to the wide-open hanger doors. The air field lay beyond, twin runways stretching from one end to the other, and he had a view of the control tower. Then a Ford SUV drove inside. The flight crew gave the vehicle only a passing glance before continuing their inspection.

Erika sat behind the wheel, with another man in the passenger seat. Raven and his team met them as they exited.

"Sorry for the delay," Erika said. "Took longer to get the gear."

"Why?" Raven said.

"The delivery was late because of traffic," she said. "Not everything is a conspiracy, Raven."

Darbo quipped, "I thought this Ford might have broken down."

Erika glared at him. "Not all Fords are prone to breaking down, Mr. Darbo."

Darbo laughed. She couldn't pronounce his last name.

Erika and the other man went to the back of the Ford. Raven ignored the smirks of his team and followed.

He examined the man with Erika. About five-foot-five, fighting fit, with close-cropped blonde hair. He had a rough face. He helped Erika remove three large trunks from the back. Erika faced Raven with hands on her hips. The Raiders joined them.

"First, I'd like you all to meet Rolf Ganser. He'll be going with us."

Raven shook Ganser's hand while introducing himself, and made the rounds with Darbo, Lia, and Roger. Ganser had a good grip and looked Raven in the eyes—a good sign.

"Rolf was a paratrooper in the German army," Erika continued, "and also a member of GSG9."

Raven was more than familiar with the anti-terrorist unit of the German federal police. He'd worked with their operatives many times over the years—in his previous life.

Ganser smiled. "My expertise is explosives."

"And he's a great drone pilot," Erika added.

"It's a hobby," Ganser admitted. "But I've been able to apply it to work."

"Good to have you," Raven said.

Erika began opening the trunks. As she lifted each lid, Raven and his crew moved closer.

"Check out whatever you want," she said. "We don't have to hide anything from the flight crew."

Darbo, Lia, and Roger inspected the HK 416s, grenade launchers, and the rest of the provided gear. Raven noted the drone in the third case—Ganser's toy. A camera equipped under the belly of the drone made its use obvious. They could use it for recon while staying concealed. Less of a chance, he figured, of being discovered while they inspected the three target areas for Mrs. Weigel.

Ganser offered to demonstrate anything they weren't familiar with, but it wasn't necessary. Raven and his Raiders had used the same weapons and equipment many times.

Raven watched with curiosity as another disturbing thought came to mind, adding yet another element of suspicion to the effort.

How did a pacifist like Weigel have access to so many weapons of war?

Or had Erika provided them through her connections?

He guessed the latter.

But he still wasn't sure. Who were her connections? Did they know anything about the mission? Would their knowledge compromise the plan?

The pilot exited the plane and came over. "We're ready."

Everything went back into the trunks. The pilot made no remarks about the weapons. Another curiosity. Raven, Ganser, Darbo and Roger loaded the trunks onto the plane. Lia and Erika collected the remaining luggage, and Raven checked the area near the vending machines to make sure they'd left nothing behind.

Lia hung back with Raven. He looked at her. She nodded. Erika was the same Erika Kruger she had met before. Raven finally had a last name, but no way to contact Oscar for a follow-up unless he found a few moments alone. With the plane full, he doubted he'd have the opportunity to call.

When the flight crew powered the engines and taxied out of the hanger, Raven felt a sense of relief.

They were on their way.
But the clock was still ticking.
And questions remained unanswered.

12

RAVEN DIDN'T LIKE FORESTS OR JUNGLES, BUT AT LEAST IT wasn't as hot as El Salvador had been. The only good thing about either environment was he never had to worry about civilians being hurt. It was only him and the bad guys.

Northern Serbia was a case of one forest being like any other. Uneven ground, fallen tree trunks, a lot of green. Leaves whispered above in a gentle breeze, and it might have been a peaceful scene had Raven and the five others with him hadn't been armed and looking for trouble. Before trouble found them.

The six hiked over a slope, Raven at the front, the others spread out behind him. They weren't in a V-formation or a staggered column; the terrain didn't allow for such a formation. They managed to keep their distance anyway so one bullet couldn't go through two people.

The flight had been long but uneventful, and Raven had been right about finding a quiet moment to contact Oscar. No dice. The night landing in an open field, without lights, had also gone without error, a testimony to the expertise of Weigel's pilots. Waiting transport trucks drove them into the forest before letting them off to continue on their own. An unexpected surprise. Welcome in any other case. Raven wanted to know who the truck drivers might talk to, but didn't want another argument with Erika. A leak could come from even the most trusted of sources, and accidentally, too; worse than the intentional leak, and Raven had seen far more of those in his life than the intentional ones. But he needed to quit second-guessing everything. If his mind was chasing too many rabbit-trail thoughts about the nature of the job, he'd fail at the objective—bringing Leslie Weigel home to her husband. Nothing mattered now but the mission.

Raven held up a hand to signal a halt. He dropped to one knee and the others followed. Darbo approached and knelt next to him.

"See something?" Darbo said.

Raven scanned the area, trying to see through the overgrowth and thick tree trunks, but X-ray vision he did not have. He had to do things the human way—stop, look, listen.

Night sounds surrounded them. Crickets predominated, but now and then Raven registered other sounds more sporadic than steady. They were invaders, sure, and the local critters didn't appreciate their presence. He understood. But Raven also had to make sure human predators didn't use the natural sounds to mask their movements.

"Making sure I *don't* see something," Raven said. They spoke barely above a whisper so their words wouldn't carry.

"Seems all right to me," Darbo said.

"You'd know."

"Sure, I'm a regular here."

Raven gestured for the team to stand up and move forward again. He checked the GPS on his wrist. They were still a few miles from the first camp, but close enough he was jumping at every sound. Darbo stayed nearby as they continued their advance, and Raven wondered if he should lower the night vision goggles perched on his forehead. They had value, but he didn't want to disrupt his natural vision yet. The others wore theirs; they'd alert him if they spotted incoming danger. The fact they hadn't suggested he was letting his nerves get the best of him.

They continued on.

THEY WATCHED the camp wake up.

Raven and his crew marched till the middle of the night, when they finally set up camp of their own to sleep in shifts. Early in the morning, before the sun rose, they started off again for the short hike to the first camp on Erika's list.

Raven watched through a break in the greenery while, behind him, Rolf Ganser prepared to send in the drone for the overhead recon.

Raven wasn't sure what to make of the camp. A row of wooden structures, a center section featuring logs for seating and some sort of lecture post / stage. He saw no vehicles or sentries. He'd sent Lia and Roger around to check another side of the camp and expected their report soon.

When he heard Lia's voice in the comm link, he knew they'd found something.

"Sam." Lia's voice.

"Go," Raven told her.

"You're on the backside. I'm looking at multiple armed subjects standing guard in front of wooden buildings. The buildings are sitting on stilts."

"Party's where you're at."

"Isn't it always? How's the drone?"

"Almost ready. Stand by."

Raven scooted back on his belly, dragging the gear attacked to his chest rig through the dirt and brush. He joined Darbo, Erika, and Ganser near a bush. Ganser had his drone on the ground, and made final adjustments on his hand-held control unit.

"Do we need to wait for more light?" Raven asked.

"Best to wait a bit, yeah," the German said. "But we can manage and save a little time."

"You'll have a low ceiling, Rolf," Erika said.

"I can work around the trees and use them for cover. The silent motors will help, too. They'll never know we were here."

"Don't bump into anything," Raven advised.

Ganser only chuckled and focused on his toy.

Raven wasn't sure the drone would provide everything they needed or even *any* intel they needed, but Ganser spoke confidently about his use of the flying machines so Raven was willing to give it a try and keep his mouth shut in the meantime.

Raven told Erika and Darbo to spread out and watch for roving patrols. They'd seen none so far; perhaps the men in the camp were comfortable enough without, or had no reason to send scouts around the perimeter because they had nothing, at the moment, to protect. Which might mean Raven and his team were in the wrong place.

Darbo had mentioned the agreement between the Serbian mafia and the assorted bandits working the forest. No patrols might have something to do with the deal. All Raven wanted to know was whether this camp held Leslie Weigel or not, but he also couldn't shake all the questions running through his mind.

Ganser turned on the drone's engines. He held the controller, and manipulated the drone to leave the ground and begin its ascent.

We'll know soon enough...

Raven watched the drone climb above the trees.

13

GANSER'S FOUR-BLADE DRONE DROPPED BELOW THE TREE LINE with only the faintest of whispers coming from the motors.

Ganser watched forward progress on the screen built into his hand-held controller, with a secondary screen, courtesy of internet mapping in sync with the drone's GPS, showing surrounding obstacles. When he'd told Erika not to worry about the limited space, he wasn't kidding. Both screens allowed him to place the drone in a prime position to watch the camp.

The video camera sent back crystal-clear visuals, but the footage revealed nothing exciting. No prisoners in the camp; the occupants numbered close to thirty from Ganser's rough count, all of whom carried weapons, none of whom wore uniforms. Their clothes looked rugged enough for the terrain, but Ganser noted nothing to suggest untoward activity. The men broke into two groups for shooting practice and hand-to-hand combat training, and while the sounds of gunfire filled the air, the camp occupants directed none of the fire at anything other than stationary targets. After practice, they gathered under a canopied sitting area for breakfast

Ganser brought the drone back and gave Raven his report. Raven suggested they get away while the occupants were busy eating.

Roger Justice had a different idea.

"Let me shoot a grenade in there for shits and giggles," he told Raven over the comm unit.

Raven nixed the idea.

"I'm sure they deserve it, but as far as we know they're overgrown boy scouts playing army and not doing anything wrong."

The team moved out.

They hiked two miles west, away from the camp, before turning north. Darbo took point this time, and they followed the GPS route to the next location.

They ran into trouble halfway.

THE BANDITS MADE the mistake of talking too much.

Darbo signaled a halt and Raven moved ahead to join him. Darbo didn't speak. He pointed. The forest concealed them from what the Armenian mercenary saw—for now.

This time, the opposition in question wore uniforms, unmarked camouflage fatigues with heavy-duty combat boots. Their weapons also matched. They carried newer Kalashnikov AK-12s in 5.45x39mm. The fifth generation AK was new, first released in 2018, and Raven figured this gang didn't have a problem with money. They marched in a line with four feet between each man. The gunners may have been kitted out with the latest and greatest, but they didn't show proper discipline. They should have kept their mouths shut.

Raven and Darbo watched the last man in the line. His AK sported a scope and suppressor. His was the only rifle different from the others.

"AK-308," Darbo whispered. "Chambered in .308 Winchester. He'll be the team sniper."

"Take him first but only if we have to," Raven said.

"Are these the guys we're looking for maybe?"

"Maybe."

Raven and Darbo watched and waited.

ERIKA WANTED to crawl under the earth. She settled for the natural camouflage around her. She didn't move, and breathed slowly, as she tracked the movement of the uniformed gunmen fifteen yards away. They talked too much. It wasn't the on-going instructions of a trainer. They spoke the useless chatter of those who had little to fear but needed to check for intruders anyway. Or they were simply undisciplined rats. She wondered if she and the others had crossed a concealed boundary; perhaps they were already deep in the gang's territory.

Were these the ones who had her mother? The longer they searched with no success, the more she had to chase negative thoughts from her mind. She'd been confident in her estimations of where her mother ended up based on the flight pattern of the jet the kidnappers used. She had to trust her gut. Her mother's life was on the line. She'd considered other destinations, but the three camps she gave Raven seemed the most likely. They'd find her. She had to hang on a little longer.

She turned her head to look at Rolf Ganser, who lay prone two feet away. He was her late husband's cousin, and she'd wanted him along not only for the value he might provide, but because he knew the full story and she needed somebody close who'd know what she was going through. Neither spoke as they made eye contact, but she caught a gleam in his eyes. The spark of a warrior ready to tear into any enemy Raven pointed at. She knew what he was thinking. *Here's where the fun begins.* He carried a pack full of explosive ordnance which included Claymore mines.

The voices of the gun crew grew faint. Erika turned back. The gunners were marching deeper into the forest, and soon she saw no further sign of them.

ROGER JUSTICE WANTED to open fire. And not for shits and giggles this time. He hadn't been joking at the last camp, but Raven would not have been happy with the American merc had he started shooting.

He flicked off the safety of the HK416, but then Lia Kenisova clamped a hand on his right arm. He glared at her. She shook her head. *She's right, dummy.* He removed his finger from the HK's trigger and let out a breath. The bush he hid under poked at the exposed skin on his neck.

They'd hiked deep into Serbian mafia / bandit territory; the gunners crossing before them were basic street thugs with military weapons. An experienced crew, such as Raven's, would cut through them with ease. After working with ex-SEALs to rescue the two girls in Marseille, he wanted to inflict more damage to the scum who preyed on women and girls. He'd find plenty of targets in the forest of Northern Serbia. The region was a hotbed of human trafficking and drug smuggling, where kidnapped women and girls were held and "processed" to the next stage of "sale" around the world.

Roger settled as Lia removed her hand from his arm. He'd get his fight soon enough.

WHEN THE LAST of the patrol faded from sight, Raven spoke into his comm unit. "All right. Let's move."

The team started forward, but Darbo wasn't satisfied.

"They're behind us," he said.

"I know. If we're in the wrong spot, we gotta keep it quiet."

"And if we're not?"

"Then it won't matter," Raven told him. He took the lead once again and the team marched on.

14

THE SECOND CAMP SAT AT THE BOTTOM OF A SMALL VALLEY surrounded by overgrown slopes on all sides. The occupants had dug a narrow passage through the western side allowing men and trucks to enter and exit. Raven thought the passage was a nice touch.

Vehicles, huts, large tents—nothing fancy or permanent. Men in camo with slung automatic rifles went about their upkeep and security tasks. The posted sentries at the largest of the tents on the northern edge suggested they guarded something of value, or it was the command tent. With the flaps closed, Raven and Darbo had no way to see inside to know for sure.

Ganser whispered over the comm link, "Drone's ready."

"Send it over," Raven told him.

"What's in the tent?" Darbo asked. Raven didn't answer, but wanted to know, too. They had to wait and watch.

Ganser's drone flew overhead as the German threaded the craft through the trees.

WHILE RAVEN and Darbo watched the camp and Ganser operated his drone, Lia, Roger and Erika kept watch for the patrol. The gun crew had to return at some point, and as Lia scanned her section of the thick forest, she hoped they'd picked the right path to watch. It made sense the patrol would follow the one well-worn path to and from the camp. Clomping through thick overgrowth wasn't any professional soldier's idea of a good time, and if the gun crew had behaved in a professional manner, Lia knew the patrol would return from a different direction than the one it left. But the crew they'd witnessed wasn't anywhere near professional caliber. They'd take the path of least resistance. They weren't used to anybody drawing down on them.

Lia and Roger borrowed some of Ganser's bombs to plant along the path via tripwire, and she hoped the blast gave them a warning. She didn't like the forest. Lia realized she'd spent a lot of the mission, so far, crawling on the ground the way she felt bugs crawling over her neck. The sooner they accomplished their mission and left the area, the better.

I can't believe what I do for new shoes, she thought. At least Raven paid well and on time, though she preferred not to dwell on the "deliver or bust" nature of their assignment. Didn't matter. She'd buy the shoes anyway.

GANSER SHOOK his head and maneuvered the drone to catch another angle of the camp. He carefully watched the screen on his controller.

"What is it?" Raven said.

"Nothing good yet."

Raven grunted and turned his eyes back to the large tent with its exterior sentries. Nobody had exited or approached. Were the sentries guarding weapons and equipment?

Darbo watched the three trucks near the passage cut into the west side slope. They were large Toyota trucks, with open beds, with what appeared to be new tires. As the men in the camp went about their business, nobody bothered with the vehicles.

"Who are these guys?" he said.

"Nobody in a hurry to do anything," Raven replied. His gut told him this was another dead end. None of the men in the valley behaved as if they held a VIP hostage.

But what was in the tent?

Until he had a clue, Raven didn't want to leave. But they were losing daylight. They'd have to camp for the night. Time was running out for Leslie Weigel; once the sun rose, she'd be on her last 24 hours before the ransom was due.

"There," Darbo said.

"Rolf?"

"Turning the camera."

The flaps at the big tent opened and a man stepped out. He called the other troopers to him and Raven, Darbo, and Ganser watched the troops gather in an informal group. The man began talking. He wore camo like the rest, but carried no weapons.

"Dammit," Raven hissed. "Boss's tent."

"Third time's the charm, boss," Darbo said. "We gotta move on."

Raven was about to agree when an explosion shook the ground.

Roger Justice yelled over the comm: "Contact!"

The patrol had returned.

RAVEN TOLD Darbo to take out the trucks. "Block the passage!"

Darbo didn't use his HK416. He unleathered the HK320 grenade launcher from his back (Roger had the other launcher) and aimed for the truck nearest to the passageway. He pulled the trigger and the launcher thumped against his shoulder. The high-explosive projectile sailed into the valley.

The men in the valley reacted to the explosion outside the camp with alarm, but when the HE round hit one of the trucks, they moved much faster.

The truck blossomed into a ball of orange fire, rocking the valley and sending the men below rushing to cover. They scattered like ants, disorganized, screaming and yelling. The boss shouted commands and ran back into his tent, emerging with a rifle and combat harness.

Darbo fired another high-explosive round, detonating the second truck in the row. The fire began to spread, rapidly, through the dry overgrowth, effectively creating a curtain of fire within the passage. Exit blocked.

Single shots mixed with full-auto bursts crackled behind them. Raven shouted for Ganser to secure his drone and join the fight while he and Darbo rushed to aid the others.

Flames from the first explosion—the trip-wired booby-trap—set fire to either side of the worn path. Raven coughed as smoke drifted in his direction. What he didn't see were many bodies. Only two mangled members of the patrol lay on the path. The others had spread out, and their weapons cracked, mixing with the return volley from Raven's Raiders. Raven and Darbo powered through. Darbo broke off to the right, while Raven slid into the dirt beside Roger Justice's prone form. Roger's HK spit round after round on single shot as he selected targets. Raven peered along the top of his rifle, lining up the front and rear sights as he searched for a target.

Lia yelled, "Incoming!"

Raven rolled right, Roger left, as the two men scrambled

to avoid the grenade arcing overhead in their direction. Raven lurched downward as the ground sloped, grunting with pain as he slammed to a stop at the bottom of a gulley.

Roger Justice spotted the grenade flying further overhead to land behind him. He kept his head down and neck covered as the blast detonated, showering him with bits of dirt and shrapnel, but none of the shards cut through his uniform. But he was still in the open. He needed cover fast. The enemy gun crew was trying to hide from Lia's rapid fire as he was their grenades. Now was his chance. Roger jumped to his feet—

The crack of the .308 sniper rifle didn't reach Roger until the slug smashed into his chest. With a cry he fell back.

Raven crawled out of the gulley, and watched Roger pitch backward. He heard the snap of the sniper's rifle, and looked around frantically to find the source of the shot. And where was Darbo?

The big Armenian crawled low across the ground, having not forgotten Raven's request he take out the sniper when the time came. He found the man with the AK .308 perched behind a fallen tree trunk, trying to line up a second shot. He had no assistant—big mistake. Nobody to look out for him while he was focused on the opposite end of the sighting scope.

Darbo's foot caught on a stump. The sniper jerked his head from the scope and tried to turn the rifle on Darbo, but he wasn't fast enough. Darbo triggered his HK416 and sent a single shot through the sniper's head.

Darbo slung the HK and ran to the body, rolling it aside, taking his position behind the AK .308 rifle. He peered through the scope and fired. One trooper down. He tracked another—*crack!* Second man down. He spotted Lia and Erika laying down a pattern of fire on two concealed enemy gunners. Darbo shifted his aim and shot one bad guy in the back; as his buddy turned to avoid his partner's falling body, Darbo put a follow-up through the second gunner's head.

Darbo then held his fire. Raven yelled for help. Roger was hurt. Darbo ran headlong to where his buddy had taken a hit.

Raven helped Roger to his feet, the American merc groaning and pulled at the tear in his camo top. The body armor below had held, but the grimace on Roger's face communicated to all that getting hit in the chest, even with body armor, was no way to have a good time. Darbo reached them, but his concerning questions were quickly settled at seeing Roger on his feet. Raven helped Roger to a tree, where Roger leaned against the trunk to catch his breath. Lia collected Roger's fallen HK.

Raven turned to Erika. "Any more?"

"Thanks to Darbo, no."

"Nice shooting, Darbo."

"Thanks, boss."

Raven looked around to account for his team. He wanted to give Roger more time, but they had to scoot. Roger understood. The team started running. Raven stayed in the rear with Roger, who kept up as well as possible.

Presently Raven took the lead and kept up a brutal pace, getting them away from the combat zone with as much speed as he could to get them as far away as possible.

They stopped periodically, setting perimeter security while they rested, and Raven checked his map. They had run from the bandits at camp number two, but they were now heading south. *Away* from the northern route they needed to reach camp number three and, hopefully, Leslie Weigel's captors.

Smoke from the fires and explosions drifted skyward well into the night, and Raven continued to smell the smoke as he stood watch over their camping spot. He stood alone while everybody else slept. Well, almost everybody…

The ground crunched behind him. Raven scooted behind a tree trunk with a hand going to the safety on his rifle. He relaxed when the dark shadow approaching said, "It's me, Raven."

Erika.

15

"CAN'T SLEEP?"

She sighed and folded her arms. "Never been much for camping. My idea of roughing it is a hotel with an open window."

"Uh-huh."

Silence. The night sounds filled the gaps—crickets, critter noises, nature going about its business despite the human intruders. Raven took solace in the crickets. It meant the bandits weren't on their tail, or *any* bandit, actually.

"Something bothering you, Erika?"

"My intel hasn't inspired much confidence, has it?"

"On the plus side, we know where Mrs. Weigel *isn't*."

"I guess."

"Nobody is talking behind your back. My people understand."

"You told me your *people* wouldn't take kindly to me."

"They must be maturing in their old age."

She stopped talking. Raven watched as she lowered her eyes from him.

"What's going on, Erika?"

"You don't get it."

"Get what?"

"There's something you need to know. Philip and me—"

"*What*, Erika?"

"He's my father. We're looking for my *mother*. And the more problems we run into, the more I think I've failed."

Raven shifted as he considered her words. He understood the situation a little more, but her revelation didn't answer all of his questions.

"Why did you hide this?" Raven said.

"It's best to let my father explain," she said. "There's stuff about him…"

"I figured," Raven said. "Why else would your mother be taken across the ocean? Your father pissed *somebody* off, didn't he?"

"Yes."

"Were you two afraid I'd refuse the job if I knew the truth?"

"Yes," she said, though more quietly than her last reply.

"All right. I'm not difficult to work with, Erika. I wish you'd been straight with me but I'll let it go for now. What we need to do is find your mother, and when she's safe we can take care of whoever started this. Okay?"

"Thank you."

"You've done fine, Erika. Give yourself some credit."

"I'll try."

"How come you didn't turn up when I checked your father's background?"

"Dad kept me out of the spotlight. He didn't want me taking any of the arrows being shot at him. You must not have dug very far, though. I'd have turned up somewhere."

I can't wait to tell Oscar he isn't perfect. "I only looked at the basics. A few pictures. I wanted to see who your Dad might associate with."

"And?"

Raven noticed a chance of tone; she sounded nervous now.

He wished he could see her face, and better judge her reaction and body language. But the night, and tree cover, didn't accommodate him.

"Nothing exciting."

"Okay."

"Why don't you try getting some rest. We'll have a hard day tomorrow making up the ground we lost."

"The fires are still burning. Can you smell it?"

"Yeah. Too bad we didn't bring hot dogs."

Erika chuckled. "Thanks, Raven."

"No problem."

She turned away and went back to her sleeping bag. Raven faced the night again, the natural noises and the ever-present shadows. He'd been right, there was more to their story, but he still didn't have everything. Maybe once they got the mom back the loose pieces would come together. Hopefully his crew would stay and finish the fight with him.

More footsteps. Roger Justice joined Raven this time.

"Ready for some Zs?" the American mercenary said.

"You in shape to stand here?"

"I'm fine."

Raven checked the glowing face of his watch. "I lost track of time."

"I overheard—"

Raven waved him off. "We'll address it in the morning. It explains why she was so eager to join the rescue effort. She has a lot riding on this."

"Get some sleep, boss," Roger said. Raven nodded, patted his friend's shoulder, and made his way to his empty sleeping bag. He slept with his rifle inside the bag. It wasn't the worst sleeping companion he'd ever had, but there had certainly been better ones.

BASED on what he saw on the map, Raven decided the best way to avoid Camp #2 and its apparently still-burning fires was to go ten miles east, then head north before making a final north-west course correction to camp three. And, hopefully, the mission goal.

It was a long trek, mostly uphill through the rough terrain, but the heavy foliage suggested their route wasn't used by any local bandits. They'd not run into further trouble, but every team member continuously scanned for danger. They avoided two paths which might have led them into another fight. They hadn't expended much ammo or explosives in the short engagement with Camp #2, but nobody wanted to use more. If they found Erika's mother at Camp #3, they'd need every bullet and bomb they had.

The long march required more stops, including one at a stream where they refilled canteens. Each one dropped purification tablets into their canteens before taking a single sip. The stops grated on Raven. He heard the clock ticking in his head, louder as time continued to run out. They wouldn't reach Camp #3 till dusk, and then their light would fade fast. He pushed the team harder at the north-west correction. This time, the terrain helped. While still overgrown, the ground was mercifully flat.

They continued at a steady pace, and then the sun started to go down. When Lia Kenisova, at point, called a halt, Raven went to her. She'd stopped at a tripwire connected to an enemy Claymore. The mine was heavily concealed by brush at the base of the thick tree.

"Welcome to the perimeter of camp three," Raven said.

CAMP NUMBER three occupied a full square mile. One side contained a row of Quonset huts for barracks, where the troops slept. A deluxe wooden shed sat off to the side. The camp commander lived in the shed. The opposite side was made up of rows of portable buildings, where "the product" —women and girls destined for Middle East slave auctions— were kept until their collection via truck. To accommodate vehicles going in and out, two lanes at 90-degrees cut through either side. An empty helicopter landing pad sat at the 90-degree point, creating a partial roundabout for the truck drivers to navigate.

The camp commander stood outside the wooden shed to look over the domain. This was a temporary posting for him in order to look after Leslie Weigel. Oliver Kohlberg had given him explicit instructions regarding their hostage. She was not to be harmed or harassed in any way, and properly fed and cared for. She was the only occupant in one of the portables; the camp's regular business was suspended till Mrs. Weigel was no longer required.

The man in charge of the Weigel operation knew better than to cross Kohlberg. Consequences would be severe if he strayed from his orders. Carl Price had been with Kohlberg long enough to have seen his wrath carried out; he wanted no part of the big man's bad side.

Price had seen too many men like Kohlberg in his career, though most of them were no longer alive. Such was the short lifespan of those who thought they could take over the world. But Price didn't mind making a few bucks off such men when he had the chance; he found it odd it was never a woman who had dreams of conquering the world, only old-timers like Kohlberg.

Kohlberg's mental state and time left on the planet

wasn't Price's concern. Keeping his own wallet full was all Price cared about, and Kohlberg was cutting checks, so why not? He'd worked for worse people—such as the 20 years he spent at the CIA. In his time with the agency, he'd done every dirty job, including turning a known and wanted terrorist into a double agent. While the politicians at home assured the American public the terrorist in question would "face justice" after a series of murders involving US tourists abroad, Price made sure the man had a steady supply of blondes and cash in exchange for information on *other* terrorists the US actively pursued. When his bosses decided the double agent had served his purpose, Price punched his ticket via poisoned whiskey. He wasn't bothered by the lies; he was a man doing a job nobody else wanted.

Kohlberg had wanted the same commitment when he hired Price to organize his sleeper cells within the US.

But for now, he had to sit tight in the forest of Northern Serbia, which wasn't terrible. He liked nature and he liked quiet. The post provided both. Maybe they'd need to keep Leslie Weigel on ice long term. He wouldn't complain at all.

Sunset. His men would be gathering for the evening meal soon. He had them working in teams of three to keep the camp secure; one team covered the immediate outside. He'd sent two others out at half-mile intervals. Tripwires connected to Claymores also promised to keep away any rescue attempt. Kohlberg warned him there might be one. His remaining force carried out tasks inside the camp itself.

The outer patrols began returning prior to dinner, and their replacements, who had already eaten, took to the field —Price heard them talking about a fire some miles away which was sending smoke in their direction. They hadn't seen any smoke in the sky from their location, but Price remembered smelling something like smoke in the air earlier. Since it wasn't coming from his camp, he paid little attention.

But he wondered if it was an accident at one of the bandit camps he had orders to avoid, or something else. What something else might be, he couldn't speculate. The blaze was too far away to have any relation to his assignment.

Right?

Price increased the patrols for the night watch.

Just in case.

16

RAVEN TOLD LIA KENISOVA NOT TO MOVE. HER INCREDULOUS expression said what she was thinking. *Duh, of course I'm not moving, darling.*

Raven talked into the com unit. "Anybody see other traps?"

"Got one here," Darbo reported. He was twenty yards to Lia's left.

"There's another over here," Ganser said. Ten yards to the right.

Lia said, "Do we—"

"Step over them," Raven said. "Be careful. These won't be the only ones."

"We can go around these, too, you know," Lia said.

Raven leaned close. "No more of your shit."

She smirked. "Whatever you say, darling."

Raven stepped over the tripwire. Lia went around. The team moved forward at a slower pace.

AUTOMATIC WEAPONS POPPED. Raven and Lia hit the dirt.

"What's happening?" He scanned the forest for targets but saw none.

Roger answered, "Squad incoming!"

Raven pulled his night-vision goggles over his eyes. Lia followed his lead. Now he saw movement, the greenish outlines of troops. Time had run out. They had to get into the camp or die trying.

Raven's crew returned fire, driving the opposing squad to cover. They stayed together, setting up a pattern of fire to shoot into divided sections of the forest. It meant they couldn't yet see Raven's team.

Raven snapped orders. "Ganser, set up Claymores. We'll drive them forward into the kill zone."

"Cover me," the German replied.

To Lia, Raven said, "Ready with grenade?"

"Let me at 'em, darling."

Raven went first, running a three-second zigzag pattern before dropping to cover. He yelled for Lia as he triggered the HK416. Two of the enemy fell to his salvo; others turned in his direction. One opened his mouth to yell and Raven sent a 5.56mm burst through his face. He adjusted his aim and fired three more rapid bursts. Lia, beside him now, tossed a grenade.

The explosive charge went off with a bang. The enemy dashed from their position, running into fire from Darbo, Roger, and Erika. The winking muzzle flashes created pinpoints of light in the darkness.

"Darbo!" Raven shouted.

"Yeah!"

"Coming to you, we'll be on your right!"

"Copy. We won't shoot you."

Lia let out a "Ha!" as she and Raven leap-frogged their way to the others, covering a short stretch, going to cover, repeating the process. Gunfire continued to crackle and split the air above them, the bullets zipping overhead like angry wasps.

"More coming!" Erika yelled.

Raven stopped midstride and rolled behind a rotted tree trunk. "Rolf?"

"I got Claymores set! Ten yards left of Erika's position!"

"Everybody fall back to Rolf. Lia and me will cover."

Raven pitched a grenade. Lia lobbed another. As the blasts detonated, they fired a string of shots to keep the opposition pinned. Raven watched enemy bodies fall, but then caught sight of the next wave behind the first.

Raven announced he was changing magazines; with a full load in the HK, he covered Lia while she swapped. They broke from the rotted trunk to head for Ganser and his Claymores.

CARL PRICE DIDN'T WANT all his men charging out at once.

He radioed the outer patrols to engage the intruders while setting defenses around the camp. He spread his men out and concentrated a force of six at the portable where they'd put Leslie Weigel. As the fight continued outside the camp border, he opened the door to the portable and stepped inside. He didn't turn on the light.

Leslie Weigel was stretched out on a cot, her arms shackled to the side of the metal frame, her feet locked to the other end. Her skirt and blouse were dirty and torn in places; the white blouse was more mud-stained now then white, and stress lines etched her face. She lifted her head as Price stopped to look at her.

"What's going on?" she asked. "You can't keep me here if there's a fight going on!"

"Afraid of bullets coming through these thin walls?" Price glanced around. The walls were bare white, the carpet threadbare brown; the windows blacked out. Empty cots lined either side of the narrow pathway between them. In normal business, they put their other captives on the cots, and filled all of them.

"You know that better than me!"

"You don't have to worry. We'll deal with your husband's little army very quickly. I have to give him credit, though. I'm surprised he sent them for you."

"You don't know my family."

Price grinned. "Try not to panic. It might get loud in the next few minutes."

―――――――

LESLIE WEIGEL WANTED to struggle against the shackles, but there was no point. The shackles held her securely to the cot. They let her out twice a day to use a smelly latrine, and fed her twice a day, too; but she waited for the inevitable abuse and rape. She knew it was coming. The type of men who worked for Oliver Kohlberg were animals; they couldn't resist a woman even in her 50s.

But, yeah, the man named Price truly didn't understand with whom he was dealing. The rescue team had been assembled by her daughter Erika. If her father was one extreme, she was the other. Both had loudly argued their points for years. Leslie feared the conflict drove Erika away at one point, and when she went overseas her fears appeared true. In the end, Erika did not stray, and even brought a son-in-law into the mix. Leslie missed Anton; it would have been nice for both him and Erika to take her away from the awful place in which she now found herself.

If they succeeded, maybe Philip would have to agree

sometimes violence was the only way to solve certain problems. Pacifist theory and hypotheticals held no value when somebody had a gun to your wife's head.

All she could do was wait and listen and hope no stray bullets broke through the wall to hit her.

Try not to panic? Nuts. As her heartrate increased and cold sweat beaded her skin, Leslie Weigel knew she was on her way to a full-blown meltdown. Because if the rescue failed, Kohlberg's goons would unleash their fury on her.

And if Erika died or was captured...

Yeah, she had every right to panic.

17

RAVEN AND LIA JOINED THE WIDE CIRCLE THE REST OF THE team had formed. They positioned themselves to spray fire at any direction the enemy might come from.

The shooting had stopped for the moment. Raven was glad for the pause. His limbs were shaking from exertion and exhaustion. The search for Leslie Weigel had taken a lot out of him and he wasn't alone. The rest of the team was no exception. He owed them big. He wiped sweat from his face with his left hand and resumed shooting position. He lay on his belly with his eyes glued to the front and rear sight picture of his HK. Darkness fell slowly, and now they faced an enemy they couldn't see. He'd removed the NVGs to focus on his natural sight; if the enemy moved close enough, NVGs made no difference.

"They've moving," Darbo announced. He was with Ganser at the forward curve of the circle. Ganser had set up his Claymores twenty yards ahead.

And they still didn't know if they had the right camp.

"They're spreading out," Darbo reported. He'd kept his NVG gear on his head. Raven watched for movement not natural to the forest environment. He watched for shaking leaves, shifting bushes; listened for snapping twigs.

Instead, he heard a voice.

A man talking into a radio, reporting no sign of the intruders after the first firefight.

Keep getting closer, Raven thought. Nobody on his end spoke. They'd keep radio silent till the fight started again.

If they turn back, we'll rush, Raven decided. A couple of HE rounds from the grenade launchers held by Roger and Darbo would be a good way to say good-bye to this crew and let those remaining know they weren't dealing with amateurs.

Then what?

They still had to get to the camp. What if they were still in the wrong place? They'd used a ton of ammo this time.

There was only one way to find out.

We need one alive.

ERIKA TRIED NOT to scratch her itchy right index finger on the trigger of her weapon. She kept fidgeting as she waited near Roger Justice. The American whispered, "Hold still."

It's not your mother somewhere in this damn forest, Erika wanted to yell. She'd told Raven part of the truth because he'd find out the family connection the minute Erika embraced her mother. It wasn't something her father had thought of, either. Like many times in her life, she'd used her father's tunnel vision to subvert his grand design.

They heard the distant voice of the enemy team leader speaking into his radio. When he stopped talking, Erika listened for a reply, but heard nothing. But the team leader's final response before signing off reached her ears.

"I think they're gone but we'll keep going till we know for sure."

Now she settled her nerves and carefully placed her finger on the trigger.

———————

CLOSER NOW.

Call it, Rolf.

Raven picked out a target, the center of a man's body. The man carried an automatic rifle at low-ready, his eyes searching the dark as hard as Raven's.

Ganser's trio of Claymores detonated one-two-three, spending their mass of 3.2mm steel balls rushing into the enemy formation. The steel projectiles ripped through human flesh and foliage. Raven's ears rang from the triple blast; he barely registered the agonizing screams of the wounded. But he still had his target. His burst signaled the others to open fire.

Raven watched his target drop. More auto fire filled the night, muzzles flashing, steam of lead cross-crossing the battle area. Lia fired at other silhouetted troops as survivors scattered. Raven shifted his aim twice, his follow-up bursts aimed at suspected targets but nothing he had a solid fix on.

"Go forward!" Raven shouted as the two-sided fight became more one-sided. He took the lead with Lia and the others falling in behind him.

No further return fire came at them. Raven began checking bodies, alerting the others to look for survivors.

"Got one!" Roger Justice announced. Then he shouted, "No!"

A rifle shot cracked.

———————

RAVEN RAN to Roger as the American merc wrestled Erika away from the survivor. Roger told her to stand down and when Raven asked what happened, Roger said, "Forget it. Accident."

Raven squatted beside the wounded man. The darkness worked to conceal most of the man's face, but Raven heard him straining to breathe, his partially stifled groans.

"We'll help you if you answer my questions."

"Crazy bitch … tried to shoot me."

"Is there a hostage in your camp? An older woman?"

The wounded man let out a choked cry. Roger Justice radioed to the team to stand by. Raven knew as well as Roger the wounded gunman wanted to yell loud enough to attract backup.

Darbo radioed back, "Copy stand-by. We're gathering ammo."

Raven asked his question again. The wounded man told him to go to hell.

"Give him some morphine, Roger."

Roger Justice took off his pack and found the medical kit. Raven moved aside to give Roger room. The American merc injected the morphine into the wounded man's arm. He rose and Raven resumed his place as the pain killer took effect.

"I told you we'd help. Now tell me about your camp. Are you holding a woman prisoner?"

"She's in…the first portable. Where we keep the other women."

"How many others are there?"

"Only her. Special orders. Only the boss gets to go in."

"How many in the camp?"

"Lot of us. Don't know total. Guys come and go."

The wounded man coughed and a little blood flew out of his mouth. Raven stood.

"Erika?"

"What?"

"Now you can shoot him."

"Get out of my way, Raven."

He did.

THE TEAM GATHERED ammo from the dead and retreated to a circular cluster of trees about 100 yards away. The enemy troops had carried, this time, a mix of Kalashnikovs and M-4 rifles. They'd ignored the AKs in favor of the M-4 and matching ammo for the HK416s. They took some time to refill their spent magazines.

They made an assault plan which included using one of the camp's trucks to escape. Several off-roaders sat parked at the end of the Quonset huts. They'd attack from the south edge of the camp; the trucks were at the north end. Getting to the portables through the open space in the center of the camp might prove tricky, and they didn't know if the enemy relocated Leslie Weigel early in the fight.

Raven ended the short briefing and the team prepared to attack. They carried weapons and ammo only. No heavy packs to slow them down.

18

CARL PRICE DIDN'T BLAME HIS MEN FOR HAVING THE JITTERS. He was nervous, too.

No matter how many battles or scrapes he'd survived, the eve before a fight brought butterflies to Price's belly. What was the enemy planning? Were they actually planning *anything*? Had his patrols truly dealt with a rescue force or had the fight been an accidental encounter with any number of local thugs also hiding in the forest?

He wondered because the attack did not continue. Why approach the camp and fight with patrols if you weren't going to continue to press? Or had the rescue force sustained too many casualties to keep going?

The hours passed and no attack happened. He moved about the camp, checking on his men, using short pep talks to keep them engaged and ready. He'd stand down at daybreak if no action took place, but he had a feeling it was indeed a rescue force out there and they had no plans to quit until they'd freed Leslie Weigel.

Price didn't know why she was important or why the

orders were so strict regarding her treatment, but it wasn't his business. He was paid to *perform*, not ask questions.

Price also wasn't sure how well the men in the camp could fight. He was only filling a seat. He'd not trained the men, or seen how they'd been taught. He did note they managed weapons well, maintained the vehicles, and kept up on exercise. But could they fight when somebody was shooting at them? Two patrols wiped out didn't fill Price with confidence.

THERE WERE VERY few problems in life, Raven once mused while drunk, one couldn't solve with the use of grenades.

Per his plan, he split the team into pairs.

Roger and Lia positioned themselves at the south end. Roger had orders to make sure he had no grenades left for the HK320 launcher by the time the fight ended. Raven wanted him to target the Quonset huts.

Darbo and Ganser covered the north side. Since Raven wanted to use one of the camp trucks for their getaway, the German explosive expert first set more bombs along their exit route to keep the enemy busy. Ganser then joined Darbo, who had his own HK320 to play with, too.

Raven and Erika planned to enter the camp and get her mother to safety.

The easiest job, yeah.

The only thing they had to do was *not* shoot at the portable buildings.

RAVEN SAID, "WAIT!" and grabbed Erika's arm as she tried to run forward. She glared at him but he didn't see the anger on her face till the first Quonset hut exploded. The orange flare of the fire shined on her face.

When the next grenade blast thundered in the night, Raven pulled her to cover with him. They landed behind a tree. Debris rained down; some chunks bigger than others. Some of the bigger chunks landed still on fire.

"You wanna get blown up?" he asked her.

"Not particularly!"

Gunfire crackled as another hut exploded and the air became hot, shockwaves rustling the foliage around them. Raven leaned around the tree trunk. The dirt road ahead, which led into the camp, ended between two of the burning Quonsets. Flames, bright and hot, ate at the metal. The fire also spread to the trees. They'd be running into smoke and fire if they entered this way. Not good.

"We gotta move," Raven said. He didn't wait for Erika to acknowledge. He bolted left, moving parallel to the remaining Quonsets. He and Erika needed to get to the far end. And, hell, change the plan—why not take a truck straight to where they were holding Leslie Weigel?

Gunfire raged; camp troops fired at the Raiders and he hoped the Raiders and Ganser had enough cover to protect themselves. The faster Raven and Erika grabbed her mother, the less time they'd spend at risk. He had to move fast.

LIA SIGHTED along the top of her HK416 and shouted to Roger beside her, "Keep those grenades cooking!"

She fired controlled bursts at the figures running through the camp. They had few places to go. The burning Quonsets cast light and shadows across the open space; she counted many prostrate forms. They were corpses; the men no longer moving. Others ran for the portables. Lia shifted her aim as fast as she could. Roger's grenade launcher thumped as he fired each round. Blast after blast knocked down gunners. Stray return fire zipped around them.

"Out of explosive," Roger said, "switching to smoke!"

The smoke round belched from the barrel of Roger's HK320. The grenade sailed into the melee. It was hard to tell grenade smoke from fire smoke, but Roger's smoke was partially colored. When red smoke mixed with the white, Raven had his signal to move in. The firing in the camp began to dwindle.

An engine surged somewhere in the camp.

CARL PRICE DECIDED PROTECTING the VIP was the better part of valor. He might turn the tide if he kept her close.

He was proud of most of the men. *Most* had stayed to fight. Others ran for the protection of the portables, but they hadn't stayed—they'd run off like cowards, into the forest on the east side of the camp. But with the heavy fire and ordnance and smoke from ever-growing fires, the ones who stayed hadn't had much chance. The attackers, however many there were, had played smart in making use of the environment. They'd counted on the Quonset fires touching off the trees.

At least it wasn't his fault the camp had a lousy design.

He shoved open the door to the portable occupied by Leslie Weigel. Slamming it shut, he hurried to her as she let out a yell.

"What is *happening*?"

"I told you not to panic." Price used a key at each shackle, unbinding the woman from the cot and pulling her to a corner. She was wide-eyed, breathing hard, sweaty; in no condition to struggle against him. She didn't stand a chance against his superior weight anyway.

He knelt in front of her, using his right hand to keep her down and holding a Glock pistol in his left. His big hand more than accommodated the thick grip of the .45 ACP Glock-21.

An engine rumbled to life. He frowned. Who needed a truck?

His men?

Or...?

19

THEY ONLY HAD TO DRIVE THIRTY YARDS, BUT GETTING ACROSS looked tough.

Erika took the wheel as Raven jumped into the back, vaulting over the side to drop low in the truck bed. Smoke drifted across the windscreen; the sweat clinging to her skin smelled of it, as did her clothes. She felt dirty and sooty but the goal was in sight.

She hoped.

Raven opened fire with his HK as she started the engine, giving the key already in the ignition a sharp twist. She flinched with every burst Raven fired. With the smoke as thick as it was, she couldn't see who he was shooting at. How did he know there was somebody there? She pulled the gear-stick to Drive and stepped on the accelerator.

Then she understood Raven wasn't wasting ammo because the truck went *thump-bump* over fallen bodies.

The smoke cleared a little as she drove forward, as if the truck was a jet descending through a cloud layer on the way to landing. She steered the surging vehicle toward troops in her path, the headlamps shining on frightened faces in the last second as troops ran away or fell to the *pop pop* of Raven's weapon. Erika kept her head low as return fire smacked into the truck's body, but not the windshield. *Not yet.* They were shooting at Raven. She panicked as his gun fell silent. A glance in the rearview provided the answer. He'd dropped below the truck bed walls to reload. Magazine in place, he engaged targets once again. *Pop pop pop.*

She wrenched the wheel right and slammed the brake pedal as they reached the first portable building. Darbo and Lia radioed they had the truck covered, but no troops approached. The enemy guns had gone silent. Raven leapt from the truck bed and ran to the portable's door. Erika watched with wide eyes. Was her mother inside?

Kwang!

The shot ricocheted off the frame of the windshield and snapped Erika from her trance. She threw herself sideways across the bench seat. A flurry of automatic fire followed, then Darbo spoke over the com. "We got him. Looks like everybody else ran off. But hurry, the fire's spreading."

"Copy, Darbo." She watched Raven open the portable's door. He entered with his HK leading the way. A pair of hands reached out from inside, grabbed the barrel, and pulled hard. The hands yanked Raven inside and swung him to the opposite wall where he crashed hard enough to make the building shake.

No!

Erika grabbed her HK and left the truck.

RAVEN EASED INTO THE DARK.

The blazing fire behind him, and the stray smoke making

his eyes sting, offered no help. He needed light. As he moved a finger to hit the switch to activate the light on the HK's Picatinny rail, hands swung around the left side of the door and grabbed the barrel. The force of the other man pulling Raven inside startled him; Raven felt himself swung inward as if the other man was hitting a home run and Raven was flying toward the outfield.

He crashed into the wall ahead. A woman screamed. He registered somebody in a corner as he kicked at the figure closing on him. The enemy's face was a shadow; the fire framing the outline of the body only for a moment in the still-open doorway. Raven twisted the HK out of the man's grasp and slammed his forehead into the man's chin. The man recoiled, Raven raising his right leg between them to kick with as much force as he could. His opponent slammed against the wall beside the doorway, his back striking the light switch, and fluorescent lights in the ceiling brightened. The shock of the light left both men surprised. They raised arms to block their eyes, but Raven saw enough of the other man's face to identify him.

Carl Price.

Price lowered his arm and gave Raven a startled look in return. They were old enemies, adversaries with plenty of bad blood between them. Raven and Price charged at each other and struck brutally fast blows, one after another. Raven landed a punch and Price's body twisted to the side. The woman in the corner screamed again as Erika entered.

"Take her out!" Raven shouted. Price faced him again, fury filling his eyes.

Erika swung the butt of her HK into the side of Price's head. The former CIA man never saw it coming and collapsed at Raven's feet.

"That works, too!" Raven told Erika. They went to the woman in the corner. Mother and daughter cried out and embraced. Raven pulled them apart, urging them both to get out of the building. Erika hustled Leslie Weigel to the truck.

Lia over the com: "We got incoming. All the bad guys who ran off are coming back and they're closing on your fast!"

"Shoot!"

"The buildings are in the way!"

Erika loaded her mother into the truck's cabin. Raven jumped into the back again as the first of the returning fighters rounded the corner ahead. He snapped out his pistol and fired as the truck sped off. Raven fell onto the bed and didn't see if his shot hit anything.

Erika knew the plan, but the bright orange flames partially covered the exit route. Enemy fire nicked at the truck. A blanket of heat, rising in temperature, fell over Raven as they neared the blaze. He curled up and covered his face. The heat intensified. The sweat on his skin sizzled dry, the noise of the blaze drowning out even the close rumble of the truck's motor. The truck thundered through. The blanket withdrew and the truck bounced over the rough terrain outside the camp's boundaries.

"One truck in pursuit!" Lia reported.

"Rolf!" Raven shouted, hoping the heat hadn't ruined his comm link. "Blow the road! We're clear!"

Raven kept low as the blast of Ganser's explosives added more fire and thunder to the night. Raven looked back as chunks of dirt rained on him. The truck sped further away. A second wall of flame and a deep crater announced the results of the bombs; no way the other team would make it through. They might make it around, but it depended on whether they braved the fire.

"Hostage recovered," Raven said to the others. "Meet us at the rendezvous."

His team copied.

Erika drove on. Raven looked through the back window.

Her mother sat beside her, holding tight to the "oh shit" handles on the dash.

Raven finally let out a satisfied breath.

Primary mission accomplished.

Now he wanted to find out the cause of the chaos, and learn the secrets Philip Weigel felt so sure he should hide.

20

RAVEN WANTED TO PUSH EVERYBODY AS FAR FROM CAMP 3 AS fast as possible, but Leslie Weigel wasn't up to the challenge of making it on foot. Good thing they had the truck, Raven decided, and after collecting Ganser and the Raiders, he kept driving. They drove until the forest became too thick for the vehicle, and finally abandoned it and continued on foot.

They found a spot near a stream to rest and refill canteens and get Erika's mother checked out. Roger Justice, the team medic, found her in good health, albeit dehydrated, exhausted, and banged up. She hadn't been tortured or otherwise harmed. Raven and his crew stood watch while Erika helped her mother trade her old clothes for items more appropriate to their situation. Erika had brought the spare fatigue pants and shirt in her pack, and provided an extra pair of sturdy hiking shoes as well.

After some time at the stream, Raven started the group moving again. They needed to find a spot suitable for an extraction, an open area where a helicopter could land and collect them. Erika had arranged the pickups. "Merc pilots," she'd told Raven. He hoped they were good and, more important, reliable.

He had questions, but they could wait. Erika and her mother needed some time, and he didn't want to bog down the march with Q&A. He needed time to process what he'd learned about the camp's leadership.

And he had a feeling he should have killed Carl Price when the opportunity presented itself. He hadn't because the primary mission took priority. What brought Price to the camp, and was he part of the larger problem? How involved was he in the kidnapping plot? Ringleader or henchman? He had the capacity to be either.

The group began following an incline, fighting through the overgrowth and forest debris, with ever-present tall trees thrown in to create their own obstacles. Darbo and Lia led; Erika had to help her mother, who kept running out of breath. Raven hung back with them, but the others didn't stray too far ahead. There had been no sign of pursuit, which was fine; Raven was happy with the idea they'd walloped the enemy good. But he wasn't going to let his guard down until they were out of the area.

After fifteen minutes, Leslie Weigel was ready to go again. Raven remained close and told the others to scout ahead. He noticed Ganser staying with the Raiders instead of sticking with Erika. She didn't appear to notice or care. Her focus was on her mother.

Carl Price. The other reason Raven felt less than able to relax despite their victory.

The animosity between the two grew from an incident involving Price's wife at the time, Taylinn. All three had worked for the CIA, and all three had been good friends. With Price gone a lot, Raven and Taylinn became a little closer than they should have allowed; their affair split Taylinn and Price apart, though Taylinn admitted their divorce had been a long time coming, and if it hadn't been for the affair, another catalyst would have achieved the same result.

But then Price tried to murder Raven. From then on, their vendetta was set in stone.

Raven and Taylinn had gone their separate ways as well, both leaving the CIA for a better life; he wondered if hers turned out better than his. He knew she'd settled in New York City, but never bothered to look her up. She was a part of the past he didn't want to revisit. Their affair had been stupid, two lonely people reaching for something neither truly shared, but they hadn't realized it until too late. And by then it was too late to correct their collision course with destruction.

Raven had been too shocked by the sight of Price, and probably vice versa, to finally settle the matter back at the camp. Neither would make the same mistake again.

"Time's up," Raven told Erika and her mother. The two women rose from where they sat and followed Raven up the hill. Roger Justice met them at the top. Below the other side lay a wide-open circle of grass. Perfect spot to land a helicopter.

———————————

ERIKA USED a satellite phone to call her chopper. Raven didn't like it. Price knew how to track such signals, same as Erika had; but she kept the call short, exchanging a single code word and coordinates with the party on the other end.

"May I see you, Mr. Raven?"

Raven turned tired eyes on Leslie Weigel. She sat on the ground under a tree. Ganser was talking with Erika. His Raiders stood watch. He could spare a few moments. Raven joined Leslie and eased down beside her. He set his HK next to him, out of her sight.

"Feels good to sit," he remarked.

"All we need is some beach chairs and cold beer," she told him.

"Are you feeling all right?"

"Your medic says I'm fine."

"You look fine to me, too, Mrs. Weigel. But people can be hurt in a variety of ways one never sees."

"Speaking from experience?"

"Maybe."

She smiled and patted his leg. "I appreciate your concern, Mr. Raven. I'm a tough bird. They did not hurt me other than to keep me shackled to a cot and confined in a room where I think many others had also been confined, am I right?"

"I don't know all the details," Raven said, "but we think so, too."

"Sounds about right. I keep up on such things. But I was the only one there."

"A prisoner we interrogated said something about special orders regarding your presence, but he didn't elaborate."

"Because he died?"

"Yup. But he confirmed you were there, which is what we needed. We'd tried two other camps and were beginning to wonder if we were anywhere close to finding you in time."

"In time for what?"

"The ransom deadline."

"Is that what my husband said?"

"And your daughter."

She laughed without humor.

"What's so funny?"

"Mr. Raven, there never was any ransom. You have no idea what this is all about, do you?"

21

THE WORDS GRABBED ERIKA'S ATTENTION. RAVEN SPOTTED HER hurried approach but kept his eyes on her mother.

"Why don't you explain, Mrs. Weigel."

"Mother!"

"Mr. Raven and I are talking, Erika. Please excuse us."

"I can't let you talk about this without being here."

"What are you afraid of, Erika? It sounds like you and your father gave Mr. Raven a phony story. We can't leave him in the dark after he and his people risked so much to get me out."

Erika stared at her mother without reply. She slowly turned her head to Raven, who waited expectantly for more.

"I'd like Erika's perspective on this," Raven said.

"Sit down, Erika," her mother said.

The younger woman joined them on the ground. She brushed small rocks out from under her.

Leslie Weigel scoffed. "Ransom. I wish it were so simple. I wasn't held for ransom. They took me hostage to make my husband keep his mouth shut."

"About what?" Raven said.

"Mother."

"Do you know the name Oliver Kohlberg, Mr. Raven?"

Erika closed her eyes and sighed.

"Rings a slight bell," Raven replied. "Philanthropist, right?"

"It's the image he sells, yes."

"I'm afraid I don't know much. I don't hang around philanthropists on a regular basis."

"I see with whom you associate, Mr. Raven."

"*Mother.*"

Leslie Weigel ignored her daughter. She kept her attention on Raven.

"Oliver Kohlberg is not the saint he'd like the world to think he is. My husband had a close association with him and I know the truth. When my husband ended their connection recently, Kohlberg decided I'd be the tool used to keep Philip form blabbing about Kohlberg's plan. And the only reason they took me is because the plan is now in motion."

"I'm waiting for the meat, Mrs. Weigel."

"Have you heard of an organization called The Fraternity?"

"Outside a college—"

"Not what I mean."

"Then no. I have no clue what you're referring to."

"The Fraternity is Kohlberg's group of rich men dedicated to bringing about a global Marxist utopia. But there's one country standing in their way."

"The United States."

"Correct. The US is his first target."

"How has Kohlberg been going about this?"

Erika continued to watch with hot eyes. But so far, she hadn't said much. Raven shifted his attention to her, then back to Leslie.

"You should look at some recent elections," Leslie Weigel

said. "Go back about five years. The Fraternity has been working very hard and spending a *lot* of money to get preferred candidates elected, from the small cities to the big ones to—"

"DC?"

"Not only house reps and senators, but plenty of lobbyists work for Kohlberg's NGOs and they work hard at pushing his agenda onto the floors of both houses."

NGO—non-governmental organizations, usually non-profit, advocating for social, humanitarian, or specific policy action. Many NGOs in the US were run by foreign countries looking for favors. They employed American lobbyists to secure those favors. Raven didn't have any particular feelings for or against NGOs as long as they were honest.

"The president?" he asked.

"Not yet."

"What does Kohlberg hope to accomplish with all these friends in high places?"

"They're sleepers. Change happens slowly, Mr. Raven. A little here, a little there, each time pushed by somebody working under orders from somebody else. But right now, they're standing by for the attacks. Their job will be to misdirect police and emergency people, or tell them to stand down. You can use your imagination. Kohlberg put them in place as the second or third phase of the plan, years and years ago. He even manipulated the voting totals when a few of the elections weren't going his way."

"And how was he able to do that?"

"He owns the companies who make the voting machines, Mr. Raven. Come on. This isn't Sunday School."

"Does this new plan," Raven said, "the current phase, involve the president?"

"Not the way you think. The goal is to destabilize the

country and force the current president out, one way or another."

"You mentioned *attacks*. What do you mean?"

"Coordinated strikes, organized rioting, stuff like that. Kohlberg's people are in the US now making preparations. The man you fought while rescuing me? His name is Carl Price. He was in charge of selecting the teams and getting them into the country."

Raven shook his head. Great. Now he needed Price alive to tell him where he put his terror cells. It was the perfect kind of job for Price. The job nobody else would want, the type requiring a ruthless and cold mind; and, it turned out, he didn't mind selling out his country for money. There were reasons his ex-wife had grown weary of him. She hadn't known of his dark side before they married; the shock of discovering who he truly was had put a wedge between them from the start. She'd once told Raven she justified it because her husband was doing bad things on behalf of the protection of the United States. But the excuses hadn't sustained her very long.

Raven finally brought Erika into the chat. "Now you. Start talking."

"Dad was worried you'd refuse to help if you knew his involvement."

"You might have asked."

"I told him to. He refused."

"Because—"

"You might kill him."

Anger bubbled in Raven's body. This was too much. He'd known something was off with Philip Weigel's proposition; he'd stayed with it out of sympathy for the man's wife. He hadn't suspected his *client* might be the true villain of the piece, or part of a larger conspiracy to destroy his country. He'd been wasting his time playing Boy Scout in the forest while the enemy within worked hard to knock down what so many had fought for and died to protect. All because of a little fat man who thought he knew what was best, and had amassed a fortune to implement his ideas, no matter how many he hurt or killed along the way.

"Based on what I'm hearing," he said, "I *might* kill him for sure. What did you father do? *Exactly*. Give me a reason not to abandon the both of you here and now."

"If you leave us, my father won't pay you."

"Erika, you misjudge me. It was never about the money. Now who's going to tell me what I want to know?"

Leslie Weigel handled the answer. "Erika was overseas most of the time Philip worked with Kohlberg and the Fraternity. Philip thinks Kohlberg's basic ideas will bring peace to the world and create more stability—no more wars —and equality. My husband hates fighting. The only reason, I'm sure, he agreed to hire you was because of my daughter."

Erika nodded. "Dad and I disagreed a lot. I'm not a pacifist. It's complicated."

"Uh-huh," Raven replied.

"My husband wanted out when he realized Kohlberg's ideas of peace was everything but. Kohlberg thinks violence is the way to achieve a goal."

"Sounds like Philip went along until the last minute, though," Raven said. "Did he try to dissuade Kohlberg at all during the process?"

"They had arguments, yes. The last argument ended with Philip leaving the group. Kohlberg responded by grabbing me. If Philip told anybody what's going on—"

"Shut up," Raven snapped. "Both of you." He grabbed his HK and walked away. Lia intercepted him at the bottom of the slope.

"Interesting conversation," she said.

Raven looked at Darbo and Roger and Ganser, all of whom stood close by, watching him.

"Ganser," Raven said. "You know any of this?"

"First time I've heard about it, Raven."

"Then why are you here?"

"I'm her late husband's cousin."

Raven was too exasperated to follow up. Then Lia said:

"I know a little about Kohlberg. He and any of his organizations are banned from Russia."

"Leave it to Russia to do the smart thing," Raven said. "I wish my country was so inclined."

Free societies weren't perfect, and men like Kohlberg had an easy time taking advantage. There was nothing Raven could do but fight them when the time came. It was one reason his war without end never stopped.

"What do you want to do?" Lia said.

"Get home. I'll think about the rest later."

22

OLIVER KOHLBERG LISTENED TO CARL PRICE'S REPORT WITH A stoic expression on his jowly face.

Price filled one of the monitors on the wall of the conference room; the old man stood with his usual hunch at the side of the table with his hands clasped behind his back and his belly sticking out.

Price finished his report and stopped talking. Kohlberg stared at him a moment before finally breaking the silence with a question.

"Do you know who Weigel hired?"

"I couldn't see any faces."

"You've heard no rumors, any talk about, perhaps, his daughter assembling a team?"

"Nothing of the sort," Price replied, "but I should add, I haven't looked. My first concern was getting clear of the camp and reporting to you."

"Where are you now?"

"Safe and out of the way, don't worry. I'm still in Serbia."

Kohlberg nodded and began to pace while he considered

Price's words and pondered his response. He'd learned long ago flying into a rage and screaming didn't lead to productive solutions. Responses had to be carefully considered and weighed against possible outcomes. He certainly required care now because his response might have unknown consequences and effect the on-going operation.

He stopped pacing and faced Price. "At this point, my plan to keep Philip Weigel from talking about our plan has failed. But we still have to keep him silent. Do you know what I mean, Mr. Price?"

"I do. If you'd like me to lead the team, I need a few days."

"We don't have a few days. Can you direct somebody who is closer?"

"No problem."

"The rescue team will take Mrs. Weigel back to the family estate," Kohlberg said. "Make sure nobody survives."

"You don't want this to look like an accident?"

"There is no time, but what we'll need to do is make it look like a drug hit, and plant evidence Weigel was in business with very unsavory people." He chuckled. It wasn't far from the truth. He continued, "If we're going to leave bodies behind, we need to give the police a rabbit to chase."

"I know exactly who to call," Price said, "and this won't interrupt our other priorities."

"Spare no expense. I don't want a failure because of an argument about money."

"Consider it done."

"Now, your next part of the assignment. You need a few days to get to the US?"

"No more than 72 hours."

"Then get over there and begin coordinating the team. We need not waste any further time talking. Thank you for your report, as disappointing as it is."

"I'll be in touch."

Price's screen blinked out. Kohlberg wandered to the head of the table and pressed a button on the console to end the connection. He left the conference room. He indeed felt sorry events had transpired as they had; he did not want to kill Philip Weigel. But the man had left him no choice.

As he walked down the hallway, his face remained blank, but his mind was busy. He'd tried to avoid getting rid of Weigel from the beginning because, at one time, the pair had been very close. He'd ordered the deaths of many, for various reasons, but never somebody who had been a friend. His usual execution orders applied to those outside the circle, people snooping to discover the truth behind what Kohlberg displayed in public, those trying to stop his plans.

He needed a drink. He was probably going to be in a bad mood for some time. But the plan was more important than any one person. Kohlberg hoped his first attempt at mercy to a traitor didn't come back to haunt him.

PRICE LEFT his hotel room and crossed the street to an outdoor café. He lit a cigarette after taking a table on the sidewalk and ordering a fancy hot coffee. He rested his arms on the table and watched the traffic and chattering pedestrians. Kohlberg's orders echoed in his head.

Another thought intruded, too.

Sam Raven.

What to do about Sam Raven.

The vendetta between them had faded from his memory as the years passed and wounds healed, but colliding with him again brought the hate back. They needed to settle the conflict once and for all. He'd not mentioned Raven to

Kohlberg for the very reason the old man didn't want him to participate in the Weigel hit. It was a distraction from the more pressing matters Price needed to attend to, but getting even with Raven was *his* priority, and he wasn't going to let the old bastard ruin his revenge.

Because Price knew Raven as well as Raven knew himself. He'd want to know *why* Price had been with Leslie Weigel, which meant asking Philip, which meant learning about Kohlberg and the whole shebang.

No way the old do-gooder would go back to his houseboat after Philip Weigel gave him the scoop on the Fraternity.

They'd see each other soon.

And their next meeting would be their last.

———

THE HELICOPTER PICKED up Raven and his team without incident, and took them to an improvised landing strip where Weigel's private jet landed to take them back to the US.

The long flight across the ocean gave everybody a chance to clean up and relax after so many hard days. For Leslie Weigel the trip was especially welcome because she had her first shower in several days. The group let her go first, but by the time Raven took his turn in the narrow stall, the water tank was low and he had to prioritize what he washed with soap and what he let water take care of. Leslie and Erika sat close during the first two hours of the flight. Erika took care of her mother's needs and let her stay in the leather seat by the starboard window.

Later, Lia and Darbo started a bridge game; Raven decided not to play, but Ganser proved an eager partner for Roger Justice. Raven liked the German and wondered if he might be willing to join the crew of Raven's Raiders. He fit well with the other three.

He liked Erika's performance under fire, too, but didn't think she'd want to join the group after the words between them. Raven wasn't sure he trusted her, either. Time would tell if they'd continue their association.

Raven spent most of the flight in a soft leather seat portside with a window and ocean view.

He was glad to be out of Serbia, and especially glad to be back in normal clothes. His body ached all over, a consequence of working in such harsh terrain, but the rescue had caused a mental strain as well as physical. He touched the locket dangling under his shirt. He hadn't been able to save those close to him, but he might save others—and worked hard to do so. He'd taken the Weigel job because he hadn't wanted to go home. Part of his reasoning was truthful. The other part? He hadn't wanted to see another man lose a loved one, even if he'd been shady with his story. The important thing, the only thing Raven had focused on, was a man's wife had been taken and he needed help. When Erika confessed her real connection to Philip and Leslie, it only made Raven more determined. The fight became personal, yet despite the mission's success he remained uneasy. The reason why dawned on him as he watched the ocean and sky meet at the horizon in the distance.

He had been trying to rescue Leslie Weigel, yes, but he'd also wanted to save his own loved ones from their fate. But they were still gone, lost to him; while Erika had her mother back, Raven wished it was the other way around. But it wasn't possible on his current plane of existence. He carried their ghosts with him; it had to be enough, for now. When he reached the next plane, maybe they'd be waiting for him.

"You look like you need this."

Raven turned to his right. Leslie Weigel held out a can of

beer. He heard his Raiders at the card table popping open cans. He accepted the can with a thank you and popped the top.

He expected Leslie to move away, but she dropped into the seat opposite him instead.

"We went off the rails, didn't we?" she said. "I apologize. Did I thank you properly? Everything happened so fast."

Raven swallowed a mouthful of beer. "Doesn't matter. Your husband will thank me when he pays the bill."

"You told my daughter it wasn't about the money."

"It's not, except when it is."

"Do you know the difference between you and me, Mr. Raven?"

"Tell me."

"When I die, I will have a proper headstone, but there will be no name on your grave. You'll fall fighting another person's war, and what will you get out of it?"

"You're not the first to tell me that."

"What about—"

"It doesn't matter what I get. I came to terms with the fact a long time ago."

"I wish it wasn't so, because we have something in common, too."

Raven raised an eyebrow.

"My life is dedicated to helping people, especially children. I get to see the faces of those I help, witness *tangible* results. You help people, too, but your way—"

"What?"

"Only ends in death. I don't understand."

"I hope you never do. It's not a proper life for anybody."

Leslie frowned as he watched her. Then she said, "Excuse me," and departed.

Raven swallowed more beer and returned to his ocean view.

Not a proper way of life indeed. But it was the one chosen for him. He'd fought against it, to no avail, enough to learn to accept his lot.

An unmarked grave.

He should be so lucky. And Leslie Weigel wouldn't understand that, either.

23

THE JET LANDED IN NAPLES AND RETURNED TO THE HANGAR they'd departed from. A car waited to take them to the Weigel estate. Erika and Ganser had to settle with the pilots, but she told Raven, her mother, and the Raiders to go on without them.

Raven watched Leslie as they sat in the back of the cushy limo. Naples passed rapidly through the tinted windows.

She said, "Feels like I've only been gone a few hours."

Leslie watched the passing scenery but looked bored. He hoped eventually she looked upon her overseas ordeal as a bad dream. She'd been lucky, really. Anybody else would have fared far worse.

The scenery didn't interest Raven or his crew; they all looked exhausted. Raven felt drained, too, but it was time to make good on his promise, pay his team, and continue the mission—on his own, if necessary. He hadn't asked Lia, Darbo, or Roger to stay, and they had not volunteered. He was too tired to pursue the question.

The Weigel Estate was a big spread overlooking Port Royal Beach and the Gulf of Mexico. The long driveway on the other side of an automatic gate carried them through an immaculate field of grass, palm trees, and marble fountains. The main house, with its multiple wings and two stories, took up the center of the property.

Philip Weigel, in a white tennis outfit with the tight shorts exposing bony white legs, waited on the porch, watching the limo move toward him.

His wife scoffed at the sight of the outfit. "Idiot. I almost die and he's playing tennis." She sighed as the limo slowed. "I suppose he's been playing to work off stress."

Raven helped Leslie out and she and her husband ran into each other's arms. It was a nice visual, but not enough to shake Raven from his quest for more answers. He'd have to remain patient. Nobody was going to talk right away.

Philip shook hands with Raven and his team, telling them thank you over and over, then turned to another man on the porch. He introduced the newcomer as his chief of staff, George Lazzar, and told him to show "the crew" to the guest house. He promised to see them shortly and took his wife inside. Raven and the Raiders followed Lazzar.

The estate felt like a slice of paradise. The palms swung lazily in the wind; the ocean waves echoed in the distance. The immaculate grass motif continued throughout the property, and Raven caught a glimpse of Philip Weigel's private tennis court. Lazzar led Raven and the others along a path to a second house. Compared to the main house, it was small, but the structure was a two-story single-family job not out of place in any neighborhood around the country. The wide path was lined on either side by more palm trees.

A surprise waited within the guest house's tiled entryway: their suitcases from the hotel they'd stayed at prior to leaving for Serbia. Lazzar explained Mr. Weigel had his people close out their bills and bring everything over. When Lazzar departed after telling them to enjoy the facilities till dinner.

THE GUEST HOUSE amenities include plenty to eat and drinks and a box of Cuban Montecristo cigars. Raven and Darbo helped themselves and stepped onto the patio to enjoy not only the fresh air but nobody shooting at them. Roger and Lia mixed cocktails and brought out the glasses.

"Sounds like we get dinner," Roger said.

"As long as we get a big check for dessert," Lia said, "it's fine."

"We'll get paid," Raven said. "What I'd like to know is what Philip and Leslie are talking about right now."

"*If* they're talking," Darbo said. He grinned.

"Ewww," said Lia.

"What's wrong?"

"Don't put the image of old people doing it in my head."

The team enjoyed a quiet laugh and the conversation faded. Raven enjoyed his rich cigar and the breeze felt good on his face. Roger said, "You're staring into space, chief. What's on your mind?"

"I'm thinking about how to take out this Kohlberg character. There's a personal reason involved, too." He told them about Carl Price. "If you all want to go your own way after this, no hard feelings. I'm not going to put the burden on you. But you know I'd value your help."

"I'm in," Lia said. "I hate this guy."

"Me, too," Darbo said.

"I'll make it unanimous," Roger added.

"Thank you. Since I'll be paying out of my own pocket—"

"Never mind," Roger said. "This one's bigger than a paycheck if what Mrs. Weigel says is true."

"I agree," said Darbo.

Lia said nothing. She pressed her lips together.

"Still in, Lia?" Raven asked.

She sighed. "Anything for you, darling. But don't think I'm going to make this a habit because I assure you, I'll never work free of charge again."

Darbo said, "Lia doesn't piss without getting a check."

Roger laughed.

She leveled a finger at the Armenian mercenary. "Don't be gross."

"But am I right?"

"I didn't say you were wrong, but we don't need to be disgusting."

It felt good to hear everybody laugh, Raven decided.

THE WEIGELS and their staff prepared a backyard bar-be-cue for Raven and his team. By dinner, Erika and Ganser had joined them, and she'd brought back all the weapons. He suggested a massive gun cleaning session later when dinner was over. They'd use the time to discuss a few things.

Weigel, at the head of the table, waited till after-dinner coffee before he addressed the group. Night had fallen; the breeze was still warm; tiki torches lit the patio. The flickering flames left a few faces in shadow, but Raven sat close to Philip Weigel to not have a problem seeing his face.

"I hear my wife told you the whole story," he said. He seemed calmer now, Raven noted, and why wouldn't he? He also didn't have any alcohol with dinner, something Erika had noted but didn't elaborate on. Raven figured pops had been hitting the bottle prior to the good news from overseas.

Raven sat on Weigel's left, and faced Leslie opposite. She waited while he gathered his thoughts to continue. Raven saw no need to press him till he was ready.

"I'm not sure what I can add," Weigel said, "but I got cold feet. Whatever you want to know I can probably tell you."

"You drew a line at violence," Raven said, "but stealing and manipulating elections you didn't have a problem with?"

Weigel looked at his plate.

"None of it was okay, Mr. Raven. We did what he had to do, for what we believed was the greater good."

"Says who?"

Weigel locked eyes with Raven and appeared ready to argue, but his expression changed. Raven waited for him to make up his mind.

"We won't get anywhere fighting," Weigel said.

"Your philosophy of life shines through."

"No need to be harsh, Mr. Raven."

"Your little gang has compromised the country, and for what? So your sleeper terrorist cells can carry out their agenda? How's it going to work, Philip?"

"The elected officials we have in place, and the people they've appointed, will run interference for police and emergency units when the time comes. Communications may be spotty, directions and orders garbled; anything to help the teams achieve their mission."

"How many cities?"

"I don't know. All across the country."

"Fascinating."

"Listen, Mr. Raven," Weigel said, "will it help you if I say 'I repent'? We did a lot of bad things, stuff I thought was justified, but now I realize my error. Okay?"

"I want everything. *Everything* you know about Kohlberg, his other connections, and especially where I can find him. Understand?"

"I do, and you'll have it. Please stay the night. The guest house will more than accommodate you all. I will collect the information for you and tomorrow morning—"

"Acceptable," Raven said.

"Kohlberg has a place in Berlin. He never leaves. Even if

you go after the others first, he'll stay put. He'll increase security, but he'll be there when you…visit."

"Good." Raven looked across the table to Erika. "What are your plans?"

"I should stay here," she said, "just in case."

"I'll stay, too," Ganser said. He sat next to Erika.

"Fine."

Raven glanced at his plate but had no energy to finish eating. He was glad to have the guest house. To have to find lodging for him and the Raiders so late didn't excite him.

He was the only one who stopped eating. The Raiders hadn't lost their appetites and finished what they had and went back for more.

24

RAVEN HAD TROUBLE SLEEPING.

Darbo was the opposite. He and Raven shared a room, and Darbo slept on his back with the covers half off and snored at the ceiling. His snoring hadn't kept Raven awake.

Darbo had the bed by the window, which he'd opened a crack, and Raven heard the faint sounds of the ocean. He left his bed, dressed, and made his way to the living room where he lifted the lid on Weigel's humidor. He selected another Montecristo cigar and went out to the patio. The night was warm, and breeze non-stop, and the ocean a little louder now. He clipped the cigar and let his mind place him at the beach. At night you couldn't see the waves, it was an abyss with sound, all black, but it still calmed him. A little.

Then another sound joined the night.

A buzzing. The sound grew in intensity.

He looked up.

Three flying objects, with long wingspans, propellers mounted in the rear, pilot seated below the wing. The estate's security lights highlighted the ultralight aircraft as soon as they dropped low enough to touch the extended glow of the lights. They swooped low as they closed in on the main house. The pilots leveled automatic weapons over the sides of their canopy baskets and opened fire. The unsuppressed SMG fire crackled through the night, bullets smacking into the house, shattering windows. The ultralights climbed over the house, and objects dropped—grenades. They bounced off the roof and started falling to the yard, only to explode in mid-air and shower the house with deadly shrapnel.

Raven dropped the cigar and ran back into the guest house.

Before he had one foot in the door, another explosion erupted at the end of the driveway. The blast was loud, powerful, and bathed Raven in a flare of bright light.

The attackers had breached the front gate.

SOLDIERS ARE soldiers and they stay prepared no matter what. Raven's suggested gun cleaning session had indeed taken place, and the cleaned and reloaded Heckler & Koch 416 carbines were leaning against the wall near the fireplace. Raven grabbed a weapon and a chest rig of spare magazines. The Raiders, Lia in the lead, ran into the room from the hallway. They'd hastily dressed; Lia wasn't wearing shoes.

"What's going on?" the Russian woman said. The trio followed Raven's lead and grabbed weapons. Gunfire crackled outside, and an engine surged—the attackers had a vehicle to go with the ultralights.

Raven didn't offer a long explanation. "We're under attack. They have three ultralights for air support."

"Should be fun," Darbo said as he readied his HK.

"Not the word I'd choose," Roger Justice said.

Raven led them outside.

The team raced into the night and dropped low near the front door. It only took a moment to see what was going on.

An open Jeep raced across the grass toward the main house, gunmen hanging off the sides. The ultralights continued to pass overhead, raising automatic fire into the structure. Raven shouldered the HK and fired at an ultralight as it flew over the guest house. He didn't see if his shots hit. But the full-auto burst of 5.56mm rounds attracted attention. The pilots converged on the guest house, and gunners in the Jeep turned in their direction, too.

Two gunners jumped off the Jeep and dropped flat on the grass to fire at Raven and his crew. Darbo and Lia fired single shots at the pair. Return fire punched through the guest house wall and front windows. Both sides were too far apart for perfect accuracy, but it didn't mean they could stay where they were. Raven felt a piece of glass land on his back. "Move out!" He broke into a run, heading for the cover of a palm tree. There wasn't much cover at all; more open space than anything; they'd have to keep up a shoot-and-move pattern and not stay in one place for long.

But the palm trees presented a challenge for the ultralight pilots. They had to avoid the tall trucks or wide leaves or risk crashing. It might keep them away from him long enough to take down one or two and swing the odds back in his favor.

Raven braced against a palm trunk. He ignored the two gunners who jumped from the Jeep. He sighted on the remaining gunners from the Jeep who had reached the porch. He fired rapidly. The wide porch had marble columns supporting an overhang from the second floor and the columns blocked any clear shots. He didn't have a chance to adjust his aim. He spun sharply at the sound of an overhead propeller, and raised the HK to fire at the ultralight zeroing on his position. Flame flickered from the submachine gun the pilot fired, but he had to shoot and steer around the palm trees at the same time. The shots smacked the ground near Raven. Raven's return fire ripped through the fabric of one of the wings. The ultralight dipped to one side. The pilot struggled to get control but Raven's next burst blasted through the pilot's head. The ultralight plowed straight into the ground.

Raven ran back to the guest house.

CLOSER! Get closer!

Lia Kenisova didn't like trying to sharp shoot under pressure. The 20-plus yard distance between her and the gunmen who'd jumped from the Jeep wasn't ideal. The battlefield was a mix of low light, dark, and shadows. In her hyperalert status, she had to focus on multiple areas of potential attack. The longer it took to deal with a threat in front of her, she'd lost track of secondary threats trying to take advantage of the conditions.

But in such cases, two heads were better than one.

"Stay with me, Darbo!"

"On your six!"

Lia left the front of the house with gunfire from the enemy shooters breaking more glass. She ran diagonally, not straight at the enemy, trying to make use of the shadows. A portion of the field ahead had no light; the glow of the security lighting didn't reach that far. She dropped to her knees and rolled, Darbo close by, both coming up on their bellies to take aim at the two gunmen. Both enemy shooters were up and moving, executing three second rushes—a quick sprint followed by a drop and roll. Lia and Darbo triggered single shots. She set her sights on the gunman who appeared to be the leader of the two. The first man bolted to his feet and ran again, stopping near a palm tree along the path between the two houses. Lia's burst only nicked the trunk. The gunner fired back. Lia triggered another round. This time she had a solid target. Her shots creased the gunner's firing arms, one round punching through; the gunner let out a scream and shifted behind the trunk.

Darbo put his sights on the second shooter. The gunner rose to start firing while he ran to his wounded buddy; he didn't get far. A trio of rounds from Darbo's HK416 ripped through his belly and chest. The gunner dropped back onto the grass and stopped moving.

Lia jumped to her feet and ran for the palm where the first gunner lay yelling for help. Darbo stayed behind her. When she rounded the trunk, the gunner looked up at her with wide eyes. Instead of wasting another shot, she kicked him in the side of the head. It never hurt to have somebody to interrogate after the fight.

"Look out!" Darbo shouted. He threw himself at Lia and took her to the ground as a passing ultralight strafed the ground around them. Another crackle of HK fire filled the night, but not from Darbo or Lia. Roger Justice fired at the passing pilot. The ultralight's engine flashed flame, trailed smoke, and the light aircraft plummeted to the ground.

Darbo gave Roger a thumbs up. Roger ran in the direction Raven had gone.

25

ERIKA HADN'T BOTHERED WITH A NIGHTGOWN WHEN SHE WENT to bed a few hours earlier.

She'd worn her jeans and a tight tank top to bed, and slept with her shoes on. Pistol and rifle remained within arm's reach—pistol on the nightstand, HK propped against the nightstand. She wasn't kidding when she told Raven she'd stay with her parents "just in case". She knew Kohlberg would retaliate for her mother's rescue. The only question was when and how. As the first bursts of gunfire smacked the house, she knew both.

Ganser slept in a guest room down the hall from her. She ran to the hallway with her pistol holstered and HK at the ready. Ganser joined her in the hall.

"What do you want to do?" he asked.

"Get to my parents. There's a safe room."

Erika ran back the way Ganser had come, passing other rooms and the fancy paintings on the walls her father loved so much. She and Ganser reached the double doors of the master bedroom within ten seconds. Erika pounded twice, then pushed through. Her parents were already out of bed and throwing bathrobes over pajamas.

"Are we being attacked?" her father said. Philip Weigel's face showed shock and disbelief. Erika didn't have time to tell him the facts of life. *Yeah, Dad, your old buddy wants to kill you now.*

She yelled, "Come on!"

Erika grabbed her mother's hand and pulled her from the bedroom, Ganser ushering Philip out as well. Erika's eyes stayed focused on the end of the hall where it met a curving staircase. They had to get to the safe room, which was on the first floor. Her father had installed the room a long time ago, an impregnable vault with room for four.

More gunfire peppered the house; Leslie Weigel screamed as the first of the grenades dropped from the ultra-lights exploded against the house. Philip Weigel stumbled on the hem of his robe; Ganser helped him up, shouting for Erika to continue, before picking up the pace and trailing after her. The staircase was only a few feet away now.

"Where the hell is Raven?" Philip Weigel asked.

Erika didn't answer. There was no time for small talk. She had to get her parents secured and get in the fight. For all she knew, Raven and the Raiders were already dead. Until she knew otherwise, defense of the house, and her mother and father, fell to her and Ganser.

But she hoped Raven and his crew *were* still alive. She needed them.

They reached the staircase and Erika told Ganser to hold back with her folks while she went down first. Her mother sobbed softly, her father trying to comfort her.

The explosion at the front gate flashed through the front windows. The house shook as the shockwave hit, and Leslie Weigel screamed as her husband pushed her to the floor. Ganser shouted, "Hurry!" and Erika raced down the staircase to the tiled entryway. She swung her HK back and forth looking for threats. Then she squatted under a window to peek through the curtains. The front gate was a twisted mess of iron, the grass near it on fire, and a gun crew on a Jeep racing to the front door.

The enemy hadn't reached the house yet, but they'd be there in moments.

"Now! Rolf, come on!"

Ganser hustled the Weigels in front of him as they began their descent along the staircase. Erika met them at the base and they hurried down a hallway to a door leading into the specially designed safe room. Erika opened the door and her parents ran in, stopping at a second door long enough to use a key pad. Philip Weigel entered the combination and let his wife enter first. He gave Erika one last glance as he pulled the door shut behind them.

Now it was time to fight. Her parents were safe in the room. They'd sent the staff home after dinner. They had no other non-combatants to deal with.

"Upstairs?" Ganser suggested.

"Good idea."

The pair raced up the staircase again and took position on the second-floor landing. Any gunners coming through the door were about to get ventilated with 5.56mm tumblers on full-auto. Erika double-checked her weapon and waited for the inevitable breach of the front door.

Then she heard more gunfire. Close by.

"Raven?" Ganser said.

"I sure hope so," Erika said.

Ricocheting rounds beyond the front door suggested Raven and the Raiders were on the scene. She heard men yelling on the other side of the door. They were taking cover behind the marble columns. She hated those things. She wanted to start shooting through the door, but not at the risk of making the enemy try for another point of entry.

An explosion of C-4 blasted the door off its frame. Debris filled the entryway, some of the chunks on fire. A wave of heat washed over Erika. Ganser shouted, "Now!"

Erika and Ganser opened fire as the gunners entered.

She didn't count how many entered as the HK416 bumped against her shoulder, but she did see one gunner fall to her shots. Ganser scored, too. He hit the last man over the threshold. The gunner twitched and fell half-in, half-out of the house.

The remaining shooters fired back as they spread out in two directions.

"We need to get down there!" Erika shouted.

Glass shattered. The sound was faint over the ringing in her ears, but she knew where the sound came from. The patio doors in back of the house.

She and Ganser reloaded on the run.

RAVEN SENSED MOVEMENT. He snapped left but held his fire. Roger Justice joined him. They flattened on the grass. The gunners on the porch took pot shots at them; when the enemy force blasted the door, pieces landed near Raven and Roger.

"We gonna follow?" Roger said. They watched the gun crew enter the house. The furious bursts of automatic fire from inside answered the question.

"I think Erika and Rolf are in play," Raven said. "Let's try the back."

"Right behind you, boss."

Raven ran. Roger followed, then shouted, "Look out!" as

the last ultralight flew over and the pilot swung his SMG over the side.

26

Raven dived and rolled as the last ultralight flew over. The pilot's chattering SMG overpowering the buzzing propeller. Raved came up on his back and fired at the ultralight's engine as the craft passed over. The full-auto burst chopped through the bottom of the cockpit basket and into the pilot's body. The pilot slumped in the seat and the ultralight continued on a straight course into a palm tree. The crash into the tree wasn't as loud as the aircraft's crash on the ground.

Raven and Roger continued to run toward the back and Roger used a wrought-iron patio chair to smash the patio doors. Roger moved forward into the dark house, and bumped into the corner of a couch.

They moved through the room to a hallway doorway. Roger checked one end, Raven the other, and Raven yelled, "Contact!" and triggered his weapon. Raven hit the floor as Roger scooted back.

The shooters at the end of the hall withdrew.

"Raven!"

Erika's voice.

"Hallway!" he shouted.

More shots cracked as the retreating gunners ran into Erika and Ganser. Raven wanted to run and help, but he'd be charging headlong into friendly fire if he did. He and Roger waited. The shooting stopped. Raven's finger didn't leave the trigger. When Erika and Ganser appeared at the opposite end, he let out a breath.

Erika and Ganser ran to Raven. "How many?" Raven asked.

"I don't know."

"Where's your family?"

"Safe room."

The four advanced down the hall, spreading out in the entryway. They crossed to another hallway opposite. Bedrooms along the hall, Erika said. They checked doorways on the right. Kitchen on the left—clear. Large dining room—clear.

Three doorways ahead. One swung open, and a gunner came out. Raven took him down with a head shot. Raven and Roger swarmed the room as Erika and Ganser covered. Raven swung his HK through the room; no other targets.

Raven pointed down the hall. "Where's this go?"

"Master bedroom."

Ganser shouted, "Get down!"

Raven hit the floor as gunfire from the master bedroom doorway raked the wall. His teammates shot back before they dashed for cover, too.

"We could sure use some grenades, Rolf!" Roger said.

"I used them all in Serbia!"

Raven crawled back to the beginning of the hall and scooted around the corner. A head popped around the master bedroom doorway and pulled back. Raven fired a string of shots into the wall beside the doorway. Somebody screamed. Raven drew back.

"There's more than one in there," he said.

Erika moved close to him. "Maybe we can find another way."

"I'm listening."

"My parents have a patio outside the bedroom. We have to get over a small wall but if we can go through the glass—"

"I like it."

"I have the keys to the doors."

Raven told Ganser and Roger to hang tight while he and Erika left the house. As they stepped through the debris at the front door, Lia and Darbo came around the side. Raven told them to stand by. Another sight caught his attention at the wrecked gate. A string of police cars with blazing cherry lights. Great. More trouble they didn't need, but a problem they had no way to avoid. But he wasn't interested in dealing with the police at the moment.

He followed Erika along the side of the house. The small patio extending from the master bedroom lay ahead. A short brick wall indeed surrounded the patch of concrete, where a small table and chairs sat. Sliding glass doors not unlike the ones at the rear led into the master bedroom. Curtains covered the glass.

Erika jumped over the brick wall and Raven followed, dropping down to scan the area for threats while she pulled a set of keys from a pocket. He turned to watch her. As she inserted the key, the glass began popping. Bullets crashed through, zipping overhead, Erika screaming as she pulled back, rolling onto the concrete to avoid the deadly stingers from inside.

Raven shouldered the HK and fired, shredding curtains, breaking glass. No need for a key now. He charged into the room, whipping the shredded curtains away from him. Three men in the room. He fired twice—one man down. Another dived behind the bed. Another appeared in the entry of the walk-in closet. Raven ducked and moved left, Erika firing as she entered. The man in the closet fell back. Raven took the man behind the bed, aiming under the mattress and shooting through the gap above the floor. The shots punctured the gunner's legs. As he screamed, Erika ran around and fired two more rounds, silencing the man's screams and ending the fight.

"Clear!" Raven shouted. "All clear!"

Raven reloaded. Roger and Ganser joined them, then they split into pairs to check the rest of the house. They searched slowly, listening, and after a few minutes determined no more bad guys waited within.

But now they had the cops to contend with.

Raven went to the front and called for Lia and Darbo, who joined them inside. He told everybody to stack their weapons, Erika to get her parents out of the safe room, and his team to follow him outside to explain themselves.

AT LEAST THE holding cell wasn't crowded.

Raven lay on the hard bench seat along the wall, Darbo and Roger and Ganser nearby; the cops had taken Lia and Erika to the women's holding cell.

Despite Philip Weigel's protests to the officers at his home, Raven and his crew, plus Erika and Ganser, had been "taken for questioning" once the cops had a look at the carnage. The gunner Lia had knocked out was also in custody, albeit at the hospital where doctors were treating his wounds in hopes of getting him reassembled enough to talk. Raven suspected the FBI and ATF were already involved in the case as well, considering the big pile of fully automatic weapons around the property, and a bunch of crashed ultralights.

Weigel promised to get his attorneys involved, but with all the elements to sort, admit, and conceal, Raven wasn't hopeful of a speedy resolution via Weigel's route. He'd need to get his lawyers working on his own issues.

Raven had another way. He and his crew would be back in action within 72 hours.

He'd used his "one phone call" to contact and old friend at the CIA, whom he'd have reached out to anyway. He explained the problem, and his buddy, Clark Wilson, promised to devote resources to the cause, especially after Raven told him about Kohlberg. He preferred not to share too much on an open line, but circumstances prevented his usual caution. He needed results fast, not cloak-and-dagger protocol.

Kohlberg's sleeper cells were on the march. They might strike at any time. The longer Raven and his people remained locked up, the more innocents remained at risk. This was not acceptable to Raven. He lay on his back and stared at the ceiling and tried not to feel anxious. It helped to devote his thoughts to the next steps in the process.

A strike at the heart of the beast.

Kohlberg.

As soon as Weigel came through with the information he promised, Raven would act.

And God help Kohlberg when he came face to face with Raven's gun.

27

CARL PRICE TURNED OFF HIS AUDIOBOOK AS THE PILOT announced their final descent to Dulles. He glanced out the window on his right, but the only sight below was the same mess of cars and buildings he saw whenever he visited DC. It was easy to see the swamp beneath the town. You could cover up the muck, but it seeped through the streets and into the people who populated the buildings and drove the cars.

Price waited patiently while the rest of the passengers rushed to unload the overheads and gather their screaming children and line up to go nowhere because the jetway doors hadn't been opened. They chattered and shuffled and made noises and he understood their anxiousness to get on solid ground, but not enough to want to stand with them and not go anywhere. Better to wait for the line to fade and sit comfortably. He had no need to rush.

His cell phone chimed, and since he'd been listening to his book via the phone—a biography of Churchill—he heard the tone loudly enough to startle him. He stopped looking at the line of passengers and read the incoming text.

Waiting at baggage claim.

A red heart emoji appeared after the end of the sentence.

Price grinned. Emma Bell was waiting for him. They hadn't seen each other in months, and he looked forward to the reunion. They'd been working hard and needed a night, or two, together.

Presently the wait ended, the line moved forward, and Price joined the flow. He walked behind the last passenger, a skinny young man who did not have to worry about bumping seatbacks. Unlike *some* of the passengers, he was narrow enough to pass through without difficulty. Price didn't bump any seatbacks either, but only because he worked hard to stay slim. The kid ahead hadn't hit 30 yet. The day he saw a balloon in the mirror instead of a bean pole might shock him.

Once off the plane, it took another five minutes walking through the crowded terminal to reach baggage claim. Another sea of people, and faces, to sort through, noise to tolerate; Price wanted peace and quiet ASAP. He wanted only to hear the sound of his own breathing. *And Emma's*, he thought.

He knew of her previous visit to Kohlberg's place in Germany. She'd contacted him to arrange the snatch of Leslie Weigel, and passed along the old man's orders not to harm her. But work chats didn't satisfy the kind of attention they wanted from one another. What she'd think when she saw the bruise on his face, he had no idea. She'd probably freak out. Instead, Price hoped she'd have a line on where to find Sam Raven.

But Raven was for later. He scanned the crowd in search of Emma.

EMMA BELL WAITED for her man away from the crowd, near one of the many exit doors, and might as well have been watching a tennis match the way she turned her head left-to-right.

There had been a time when she considered the Fraternity the best thing to ever happen to her. When she met Carl Price, he became the first; the Frat fell into second place.

It was hard being over 30 and still single. She'd given up hope of finding a decent guy in a sea of losers and men only interested in hooking up for a night or two and moving on to the next fling. Washington, DC, was full of those, young bucks in the diplomatic corps or other areas of government and media who saw life as one big party because they were still young enough not to understand every party ends. But end it would. For Emma, having never been a party girl to begin with, she'd never fit with the scene and it affected her love life to the point where she spent most of her time alone.

Her boss, Arthur Hunt, assigned her to work with Carl as soon as the renegade CIA man joined the Fraternity. He was hired to take on the odd jobs and carry out the dirty tricks required for Kohlberg's master plan. The relationship soon blossomed into more than agent / handler; they'd become lovers, and found in each other kindred spirits who wanted to work for a common good.

But six months apart…

Kohlberg had jobs for them to do, and while Emma's kept her at CIA headquarters and around DC, Carl had to spend most of his time overseas or elsewhere in the US. His recent project, organizing the sleeper cells, had been extra dangerous; she'd feared he might come to the attention of the FBI. Kohlberg had people seeded within the FBI, but it wasn't a guarantee. If a group of agents without affiliation began an investigation, the boss had an insurance plan. But it remained a mystery. Emma wasn't sure what the plan entailed. She almost didn't want to know. So far, they'd been lucky. She hoped the luck didn't run out.

When she spotted him, she didn't hesitate. She called his name and waved, raising her right hand over her head, moving it back and forth, laughing like a schoolgirl, and she didn't care. She ran across the smooth floor to him and launched herself into his arms; like a champ, he grabbed her, dropping his carry-on tote bag first, and she relished the tight squeeze he gave her trim body. He set her down.

"Finally!" she said.

"Let's get my stuff and get out of here."

"Then what?" She grinned.

"Do you have to ask?"

PRICE FELL on her like a tree trunk but gave her time to catch her breath while he worked on her clothes. She wondered if she should have made the bed and tidied the room; she expected Price didn't notice or care about the mess.

The problem with women's clothes, Emma always said, was all the buttons and straps made quick release difficult unless you went without a key piece.

She raised her rear end to help him get her slacks off and then had to hurry and kick off each shoe because he forgot those. While he tossed her slacks on the floor, she slipped off her bottoms and didn't have to worry about her blouse for a bit because he dived between the V of her legs and began probing and kissing and licking and she tried to speed things along by fiddling with her blouse buttons but by the time Price started she felt weak and silly all over and decided the hell with it he'll get to 'em in a second let's lay here and enjoy it...

CARL PRICE WAS on his second cup of coffee, having finished his eggs and sausage, when he finally talked to Emma about what happened during the Leslie Weigel situation. She faced him across the kitchen table and listened without comment. Kohlberg had not updated anybody on the details, and it was all news to her. She wasn't surprised by the old man's silence, though. It was Kohlberg's way. But now, she supposed, she needed to know since she was Carl's handler and also needed to tell Arthur.

Carl ended his story describing the raid and rescue and the appearance of Sam Raven.

"Do you know him?" he asked her.

Instead of coffee, Emma drank tea; she sipped her mug and shook her head.

"I don't *know* him, but he is a known quantity around the building. He's a love or hate type, no in between. Every now and then he does an odd job for somebody named Clark Wilson."

"You work with Wilson?"

"He's in special ops. Different department than me."

"If Raven was hired to get the woman back," Price said, "it's a good bet Mr. Weigel has told him about Kohlberg and the plan."

"Does Kohlberg know about Raven?"

"I explained everything. His orders are to continue as we've planned. I need you to look for Raven and see if you can find him. He'll try and stop the operation, and he'll do so by coming after *me*." He explained the vendetta between the two of them, and how Raven wouldn't stop until he found Price's sleepers and then Price himself.

Emma looked worried. "I'll do whatever I can, of course."

"Be discreet. He has friends. In fact, do what you can to

monitor Wilson, too. They'll be in touch if they haven't spoken already."

"How long till you leave?"

Price drank some more coffee. "I can fudge another day."

"Good. So can I."

He smiled. She smiled, too.

28

RAVEN STOOD WHEN THE GUARD CALLED HIS NAME.

He exited the holding cell, and the guard cuffed him. A second brute holding a nightstick watched. Even with his considerable fighting prowess, Raven recognized fellow experts when he saw them. The two guards were not men to mess with.

The guards led Raven down a hallway to another room where they opened a steel door with a small square window. They shoved him inside. The door slammed shut with force. Raven stumbled from the shove but didn't fall.

A cold interview room. Table, two chairs, and a sour-faced man. The man at the table. He wasn't a cop. He didn't fit in with the rest of the jail personnel.

"I get the feeling," Raven said, "they're mad."

"Oh, buddy, they are *pissed*," the man said.

"My apologies for not shaking hands, Clark."

"Ha!" Clark Wilson said. "I can't believe they left the cuffs on after the heat I brought down. You have the full weight of the State Department behind you, Sam. You're to be released immediately on the grounds of national security. Or something. I kind of made it up as I went along."

Raven kicked the empty chair out from the table and sat without difficulty, but he had to sit on the edge so as not to smash his arms behind him. He looked around with a raised eyebrow and mouthed "camera". A small unit with a lens was mounted in a high corner behind Wilson. The CIA man shook his head and tapped his watch. He wore a special time piece which emitted a jamming signal. The signal blocked audio transmissions. The guards, and any detectives, watching the video to learn more about the prisoner and their mysterious guest had no way to hear the conversation.

"We have two hours before they let you out," Wilson said. "Tell me what's up."

Raven and Wilson shared a long history. Both had served at the CIA until Raven's exit, and Wilson had also been a capable field operative. Starting a family made him switch to a desk job at headquarters, but doing so hadn't dulled his edge. He currently served as a Senior Operations Officer for the Special Activities Center.

Raven told his side of the story in greater detail than earlier. He covered Leslie Weigel and Serbia and the entire mess, including his encounter with Carl Price.

Wilson knew Price only by reputation, but was well aware of the conflict between him and Raven. He admitted the Agency kept an eye on Price now and then, but only had a cursory interest in his activities. "But it sounds like we should take a closer look," he added. "Do you think he might be the best way to find Kohlberg's sleeper cells?"

"I have no doubt he assembled the teams himself," Raven said. He shifted. The cuffs and position of his arms caused an ache. "He's my second choice, though."

"You want to go straight for Kohlberg?"

"He'll have all the information on the sleepers, and he

apparently never leaves his home in Berlin. Philip Weigel can suggest where the sleeper cells are based on the elections Kohlberg manipulated, but we'll be playing whack-a-mole. Kohlberg will have the master list from which we can round up the suspects."

Wilson nodded. "We can't waste time chasing Price, yeah. As much as you might like to."

"I'll settle with Price," Raven said. "He won't be forgotten."

"All right. Let's call the guard and get you back to the cell while they process you out. Are you making your own travel arrangements or may the CIA contribute?"

Raven shook his head. "It's best if I move on my own. If Kohlberg has people at the Agency, they'll catch on and tell him. Hell, I'm surprised you made it here without difficulty. And I don't want a target on *your* back, Clark."

"You always do this, Sam."

"Do what?"

"Take all the responsibility yourself."

"You have a family to think about."

Raven tried never to dwell on the matter, but Wilson had what Raven lost. He wasn't going to put his friend, or Wilson's wife and children, in harm's way.

"Sam—"

"End of discussion. My team and I will handle this, but we'll be in touch if it goes sideways."

"Okay."

Wilson rose form his chair and helped Raven to his feet. Wilson yelled for the guards, one of whom opened the steel door.

Both guards took hold of Raven. He said to Wilson, "I owe you one, pal."

Wilson grinned. "Make it two or three by now, champ."

Two hours turned into three but eventually the police released Raven and his team into Wilson's custody, and they returned to the Weigel estate.

Weigel brought in a cleanup crew to finish what the cops and Feds started, but repairs to the house weren't getting done overnight. In the bright sunshine of the afternoon, Raven finally saw how much damage the fight had caused. Pock marks and holes dotted the main house; the guest house was out of commission for the foreseeable future, as it needed new windows, a new door, and many other repairs. Erika joked the main house was big enough they could close off the damaged portions and be none the wiser.

Raven noted she kept up her sense of humor; she'd shown very little humor while the enemy held her mother captive. But the wary look on her face, and in her eyes, showed real stress despite the brave façade.

She still wanted to remain behind to protect her parents, and Raven convinced the family to relocate to an area unknown to Kohlberg. Philip Weigel promised he had such a place in mind.

Weigel also handed over the information Raven asked for regarding Kohlberg, which Raven had to admit wasn't much. Weigel hadn't been privy to every discussion, but he did prove valuable on the rigged elections orchestrated to put Kohlberg representatives in positions of power.

But Raven remembered his comment to Wilson about more traitors in the ranks of law enforcement, the CIA, and elsewhere. He decided to hold onto the data. For now, stopping the sleeper cells was first priority; there'd be time to sort out the remaining players after.

Erika provided transport to Germany with a local flight outfit willing to make the trip—more of her "connections" at work—as well as the trunk of weapons they'd used in Serbia. Once again, she was proving to be an impressive asset despite how their association began, and Raven was willing to overlook the rough start. He wanted to find out, when the dust settled, if she'd throw in with his gang for more action in the future. Because Kohlberg was certainly not the last of his kind, and the good guys needed all the help available.

29

Lia Kenisova took the seat across from Raven. The drone of the jet engines filtered through the cabin, but did not disturb the movie Darbo and Roger watched at the front end of the cabin. Raven sat alone in the back, staring out a window, but turned to Lia when she sat and crossed her legs.

"You've been quiet," she said. "Everything all right?"

"In the grand scheme, is anything really ever *all right*?"

"Don't give me your usual guarded crap, darling. What's bothering you?"

"I'm not sure myself," Raven said, "but something *is* nagging at me. I can't articulate what yet."

"Something about Kohlberg?"

"How can a guy never leave his house?"

"He's a known figure around the world," Lia said. "He's not going to hide like the usual riff raff you deal with."

Raven chuckled. "Riff raff isn't quite strong enough to describe him, I'm afraid."

"It's too good to be true, isn't it?"

"What do you mean?" Raven said.

"We've been handed a bad guy on a plate. No investigation, no search for proof, none of our usual due diligence. We're going to Germany to whack a guy and steal information on these sleeper cells and get outta there."

"You might have hit on what's nagging at me."

"But we don't have time to figure things out. If we take too long, the attacks begin. Or whatever those cells have in mind."

"Very astute."

"You didn't bring me along for my sparkling personality, darling."

"Here's what I have no doubt of. One, Weigel is telling the truth. Two, his wife was kidnapped. Three, when we rescued her, a group of very well-armed bad guys tried to kill the entire family. It's as if Kohlberg was doing Weigel a favor for old time's sake, and when it didn't work as planned, he said the hell with it and attempted what he probably should have done from the start."

"Sounds like we have all the evidence we need," Lia said. "What's the problem?"

"I'm used to working for it, not getting every detail handed to me."

"Or?"

"I'm not sure what else. *Something*."

"We land in a few hours. If you don't think of it soon—"

"I'm sure it will bite us in the ass, yes."

Lia smiled without humor.

RAVEN DID NOT like the look of the Kohlberg estate. His shoulders sank with invisible weight as he examined the layout through a pair of binoculars.

"I don't like it, either," Darbo said. The Armenian mercenary lay next to Raven. They were on the ground across the road from the main entrance, atop a small rise. The stone wall encircling the property loomed large.

"No countermeasures on the wall," Raven said. "The top of the wall looks about four feet across."

"Try six," Darbo said. "Two people can stand side-by-side."

"But you confirm no barbed wire or other deterrents?"

"Who needs 'em when you have the huge lawn to cross," Darbo said. "The countermeasures are buried under the grass. Motion sensors connected to lights, maybe mines with mild explosives, enough to maim but not kill—I have a feeling Kohlberg likes live prisoners he can torture to death. How many guys with guns you count?"

"Since we've been here, they work in shifts of five and the others go inside or to the servant's quarters."

Raven lowered the binoculars. He let out a deep breath as he looked at the estate with his own eyes. The night was cold but they were both dressed for the chill.

"What's on your mind, boss?"

"Row of buildings to the right of the main house."

Darbo looked again through his binoculars and adjusted his focus. "So?"

"It's not 500 yards from the wall to one of those. They probably buried countermeasures under the grass. Running that distance is stupid. But those buildings are much closer to the wall."

"Do you really want to go over the wall there? You know who's in those buildings? Staff and gunners? Get it, boss?"

"Just me. The rest of you stand by. Somebody cuts power to the house, I start keeping the gunners busy, and the rest of you move in."

"Who cuts the power at the junction box?"

"Let's get back to the others and flip a coin."

"I love how you consider every detail, boss."

"By the time everybody who's sleeping reacts, we'll be in the house."

"If you say so, boss."

Raven and Darbo scooted from their positions and hurried back to Lia and Roger.

RAVEN DROPPED over the top of the wall and landed on soft grass.

He ran twenty yards to the first building and dropped flat at the base. A row of windows looked out toward the wall he'd come over, but no lights burned within. It appeared thick drapes covered the windows, probably to accommodate day sleepers. Raven spoke into his comm unit.

"I'm over the wall."

"Copy, boss," Darbo said.

"Be aware of potential non-combatants inside the house. There might be overnight staff."

"Copy."

Roger said, "Patrol heading your way."

"Where?"

"They'll be coming around to you in a few seconds."

Raven moved fast, reaching the corner, a solid wall with no windows. The entrance to the building waited around the other side. Raven squatted and faced the way he'd come. He wanted to be face-to-face with the patrol when they came around. He took out his pistol and clicked off the safety. A suppressor extended from the muzzle. He didn't want any shooting this early, but if the enemy was going to get this close, he had no choice.

The rumble of the electric vehicle reached his ears. Roger hadn't mentioned such a vehicle. Two people in a golf cart. The little machine might come in handy. The cart turned the corner. A spotlight on the dash shined on Raven, and he brought up an arm to block the glare. The driver stomped the brake, the passenger going for a gun, and Raven fired. His first one-two combo pinned the passenger to the seat, two shots in the chest; the gunner released his weapon and slumped. The driver never had time to dig his own weapon out. Raven's second pair ripped a chunk of flesh from his neck and drilled through the side of his head.

The .45 trickled smoke as Raven ran to the driver. He hauled out the body. The weight keeping the brake engaged, once removed from the pedal, made the cart lurch forward. Raven jumped behind the wheel and stopped the cart. He pulled up the emergency brake and then shoved the passenger's body onto the grass. He kept the man's submachine gun and started driving forward again.

"Got transport and heading for the house," Raven reported. "You might have mentioned the golf cart, Roger."

The cart bounced along. He aimed for the rear of the main house.

No reply from Roger.

"Rog? Anybody?"

The comm link remained silent.

"Mr. Raven."

A voice he didn't recognize.

"Stop the golf cart, Mr. Raven."

Raven did as ordered, but nobody had told him to stay seated. He left the cart and dropped low near the back for cover. But he had no idea where the unknown speaker was watching from; he might still be exposed.

"Who is this?" Raven asked.

"Get back in the cart."

"Who are you?"

"Get back in the cart, Mr. Raven. I want you to travel to the north end of the property. If you do not, we will kill your people one at a time, and see you're trapped in a cross-fire from which you will not escape."

Raven blinked. He thought back to his chat with Lia on the plane, his fear of something he had no means to identify, something to bite them in the rear.

"Ouch," Raven said.

"Repeat."

"Nothing. Do not harm my people." He climbed back into the cart. "Heading your way now."

Raven steered north—toward the rear of the property. Shadows enveloped him when he left the glow of light around the house. He watched for the wall.

"Shall I jump over?" he asked his unknown friend on the comm link.

"Yes, and no tricks. You'll have more guns on you than you can see. We want to do this quietly, Mr. Raven."

The cart bounced as Raven drove.

30

"HEADS UP, LADIES."

Raven tossed his captured submachine gun over the wall, then used the golf cart to boost his jump over. He landed on both feet but the uneven ground upset his balance. He dropped to his knees before he fell over. Three men aimed rifle muzzles in his face.

Raven rose, raising his hands to his shoulders.

A man moved behind Raven and shoved him forward. The others in front parted and helped escort him up a rise to a cluster of sweet-smelling pines. Roger Justice and Lia Kenisova rested on their knees with a large man standing over them. The man grinned at Raven; he was dressed in full combat gear, as were his men, but he held no weapon. The only firearm Raven noted was the pistol the man wore on his right hip.

"Mr. Raven," the man said.

"Howdy."

A blow to the middle of his back knocked the wind out of him. Raven dropped to hands and knees, gasping and coughing. When he stopped, he made eye contact with Roger, and hoped telepathy was real.

Where's Darbo?

Roger only shook his head.

Which meant what? Raven had heard no gunfire, so he figured Darbo still moved among the living. Unless suppressed gunfire had taken him out. But none of the weapons pointed at him had suppressors attached.

"You know me." Raven shifted his eyes to the man standing near his teammates. "Who are you?"

"Nobody."

At least Raven knew he was the one who took over the comm link; had he taken Darbo's unit? He tried to see if Roger and Lia still wore theirs, but in the dark, he had no way to tell.

"A Kohlberg stooge, huh?"

"You won't be around long enough to care who I am."

"Shooting us out here might wake up the neighbors."

"The nearest is ten miles away. We are quite isolated."

No mention of suppressors...they weren't worried about noise... Had Darbo survived?

"You're American," Raven said.

"So?"

"I expected an accent, is all. It sounds like Kohlberg isn't very diverse in his hiring practices. Tell me, does he have the required number of POCS, Bi-POCS, and non-binary they/thems?"

"You're not making sense, Mr. Raven."

"I'm only trying to make sure the LGBT-PD doesn't come and cancel your boss for being a bigot. They have their own covert action squad. Surprised you didn't know that."

Nobody chuckled.

"All right, let's get this over with then," Raven told him.

"The ground ain't helping my poor arthritic knees none. You got all three of us."

Another test.

"You made a good effort, Raven," said Nobody. He reached for the pistol on his hip.

The first shot whispered overhead on Raven's left; the distant *crack* followed, and Nobody doubled over with a hole where his right ear had been. He collapsed. Another shot took down one of the men who'd escorted Raven from the wall. Raven rolled left, drawing the .45 they'd neglected to take, and used it on the other gunners standing behind him. They didn't know who to shoot, the prisoners running for cover, or the unseen sniper, and as Raven's .45 barked again and again and Darbo's precision fire continued, soon it didn't matter. Raven and Darbo cut them down without mercy. Raven scanned for more targets. Roger grabbed him and pulled Raven away.

"How'd they miss Darbo?" Raven said. Roger and Lia gathered their captured weapons from where Nobody stacked them.

"The question is how they found *us*," Lia snapped.

Darbo's voice crackled in Raven's ear. "Okay, boss?"

"No holes we weren't born with; where you at?"

"Thirty yards left. Near the junction box I was supposed to blow."

Darbo had drawn the straw to kill the lights.

"Comin' to you." Raven took the lead and Roger and Lia ran after him. They left the dead bodies behind. *Let Kohlberg tend to his stooges*, Raven decided.

———————

HANNO, the man in charge of Kohlberg's security, paced with nervous tension etched in his angry face.

"All of them?"

One of the house guards stood in the doorway of the first-floor room.

"Yes," the guard said. "And one of our patrols."

"I *told* him this wouldn't work!"

"But they did—"

"They kept this Raven fellow from getting into the house, yes."

"Do we tell Mr. Kohlberg?"

"I'm not waking him up. We need to find a way to make this work for us before I tell him. Okay, back to your post."

The guard departed.

Before he spoke with Kohlberg in the morning, Hanno wanted a new plan squared away. He wouldn't wake up the boss, but he had no problems waking up somebody across the world in the United States.

Then again, considering the time difference, Arthur Hunt was probably already awake.

Hanno dug out his cell from a back pocket and dialed the CIA man.

"Everything okay?" Arthur Hunt answered on the first ring.

"Your people are dead."

"*What?*"

"The team you sent. Raven killed all of them."

"This is awful."

"We can use this to our advantage," Hanno said, "if you can make certain suggestions to those in charge."

"Raven has friends here—"

"Explain it to them. If Raven isn't taken off the field, the entire plan is in jeopardy."

"Does Kohlberg know?"

"Not yet. He'll know first thing in the morning. It might be nice to give him some good news along with the bad."

"I'll get on it, Hanno. But it may expose me."

Hanno laughed. "Pretty soon we'll be in charge, and it won't matter, Arthur."

"All right."

They hung up. Hanno let out a breath. It would be nice to call it a night and get some rest, but his work wasn't over. He had to figure out how to get rid of the bodies Raven left behind.

IT WASN'T the best safe house, but Raven didn't plan on being there long. They were too close to neighboring houses, though they had a lot of space between the homes. They'd chosen the location because of its close proximity to the Berlin-Brandenburg Airport. The flight crew who'd brought them to Germany had gone back to the US, so Raven's flight crew from Stockholm was on the way to collect them. They only needed the house until the jet arrived. Raven figured they had another few hours, long enough to sleep and regroup from the disaster at Kohlberg's place.

Raven slept a few hours, but a vivid dream he no longer remembered woke him. After lying in bed a few more hours, he rose to shower and dress and went to the kitchen to make a cup of tea. He sat at the kitchen table, enjoying the quiet, and stared into space.

He didn't want to leave Berlin without having accomplished the mission, but he needed a new approach, one he probably should have taken at the beginning. He'd wanted to catch the big fish and end the threat, but he'd blown the opportunity because the other side had planned for his exact move. Because they knew he was coming. They'd known from the git-go Clark Wilson was springing him and his team from jail; they'd let it happen; it was a set-up to get rid of him in Berlin. He'd wanted to keep Clark out of the line of fire. Too late. Clark already had a target on his back.

Now he needed an alternate route to victory, and the road led through Carl Price.

Via his ex-wife, Taylinn.

Raven had doubts about going to Taylinn, though. Their history, for one. He also didn't want to involve a civilian in a matter she need not be exposed to; at the same time, if she knew what Carl was doing, she might volunteer to help stop him. He had to ask. Explain the risk. Even talk her out of helping. Whatever she decided would be her decision, not the result of him manipulating her emotions.

His cell rang. The phone sat on the table next to the still-steaming mug. Clark Wilson's name flashed on the screen. Raven answered.

"Clark?"

"What the hell is going on over there?"

"They knew we were coming, Clark. They knew from the beginning."

"And now it's worse, Sam. Berlin Station has an alert out for you and your people. What happened at Kohlberg's?"

"You want my side, or do you already know?"

"Sam, those shooters were CIA."

Raven slowly rose from the chair and began to pace the dark living room adjoining the kitchen.

"Clark, I had no idea. They had us dead bang."

"Here's what I've been able to learn," Wilson said. "Somebody here at headquarters, I'm not sure who yet, sent shooters to cover Kohlberg."

"Price told his boss about me; Price is working with somebody at the Agency—"

"Who has the power to put you on a list."

"What does Berlin Station want?"

"For now, a conversation. But they're throwing the works at you if they get you."

"They can talk to me if they catch me. Has Fisher weighed in?"

Christopher Fisher was Wilson's boss. As Director of Operations, Chris Fisher oversaw missions carried out by the Special Activities Center and it's two sub-groups, Ground Branch and Special Operations Group.

"Fisher is trying to get to the bottom of this, too," Wilson said. "It's not something he signed off on."

"Seems like a small circle of suspects."

"Sam, I swear, we're *working* on it. We want answers as badly as you do."

"If the CIA is looking for me, I need to get off this phone and out of Berlin, yesterday," Raven said. "I'll get back with you when I'm sure it's safe. Watch your back."

"You, too."

Raven hung up. He didn't want to wake up the Raiders but he had no choice and it was part of the reason he paid them so well.

A noise broke the silence. Raven stood in the dark living room and listened.

The noise grew louder.

A high-pitched whine. More than one.

Motorcycle engines.

HAD THEY TRACED HIS PHONE? MONITORED CELL conversations to pick up his voice? Raven cursed. There were a number of ways the CIA could track him and Berlin Station or not, *conversation* or not, he didn't think a group of motorcyclists running all-out in the middle of the night meant anything but trouble.

Raven ran through the kitchen, slapping the switch to turn out the light. He shouted and banged on doorways to wake up the Raiders. Reaching the bedroom at the end of the hall, the one he'd used, Raven grabbed his shoulder rig with the Nighthawk Custom .45 nestled in the holster. He met his three teammates in the hallway as they hurriedly dressed and his only were of explanation were, "Attack incoming!"

He ran back to the front of the house, aware he'd look foolish if he guessed wrong.

The motorcycle engines enveloped the house as Raven reached the front room. He cut left through the kitchen to the adjoining family room, where sliding glass doors led to the patio. An object crashed through the front kitchen window and bounced off the stove. The object clattered onto the linoleum floor.

Hate it when I'm right! "Grenade!"

The blast ripped apart the kitchen, Raven rolling over a couch as debris flew into the room. A piece of the mug he'd poured his tea into landed two inches from his face.

Gunfire replaced the noise coming from the motorcycle engines, bullets punching through walls and glass, striking the interior with fury. Bits of sheetrock and miscellaneous debris rained down, Raven keeping low and waiting for the next phase when the shooters stormed the house.

Over the rattling automatic weapons' fire, Darbo shouted at Lia and Roger: "Find cover! Don't get stuck in the hallway!"

The shooting stopped. But then...

The motorcycles buzzed to life once more. Raven frowned and crawled to the edge of the couch to peek around. The attackers lobbed two more grenades through the gaps in the kitchen glass, but they weren't high explosive. The grenades were thermite. The containers burst and spread super-heated gas across the floor. They weren't going to storm the house; they wanted to burn it down.

"Everybody out!" Raven shouted as he blasted the patio door glass. He didn't pause to see if the Raiders heard him.

He ducked through the broken glass and ran outside, following a paved walkway to a side gate. He climbed over the fence, wincing at the shock recoiling through his legs as he landed on the opposite side. He ran to the front with the Nighthawk in hand. Four men in leather jackets, with helmets, armed with auto-rifles, straddled dirt bikes. As they turned away from him to flee the scene, Raven braced the .45 in both hands and fired twice.

The biker in the rear fell off his two-wheel machine and the bike tipped over with the engine chugging. Raven stowed his gun, uprighted the bike, and swung onto the seat. Fire blazed within the house; he spotted movement in the bike's right mirror and turned back. Darbo, Lia, and Roger, using the same escape path he had, came around the front. Raven tossed them a wave and ignored Roger's yell. He gunned the engine and took off after the other three bikers. The enemy rode with weapons visible. Their staging area had to be nearby. Raven downshifted and increased speed. Cold wind beat at his sweaty face, but he didn't care. His attention remained on the red tail lights ahead.

ROGER JUSTICE YELLED to keep Raven from going, but the boss took off with the motorcycle's engine loud in Roger's ears.

"You're nuts!" he shouted at Raven's back.

"So are we," Darbo said, "if we don't scoot. We're all over the police band by now."

Thick smoke plumed from the gaping holes in the house; they coughed as they ran to their SUV, parked on the street. Darbo started the motor once they trio piled inside.

"Where we going?" Lia said from the passenger side. Roger clicked his seatbelt in the back.

"We follow the boss! Get the guns ready!"

THE BIKER in the lead charged ahead, while the other two twisted back to fire at Raven. The flashing muzzles might have caused concern, but they rode solo, and had no ability to aim and ride at the same time. They were wasting shots. One gave up and surged to catch up with the leader. By the time the third gave up and followed his partner, Raven had them all in sight. The leader pulled into a junk yard of stacked and wrecked automobiles. Raven turned onto the driveway as the three bikers entered an open garage.

Raven slowed his bike and swung off as aimed gunfire snapped his way. Raven rolled to cover behind a wrinkled fender. Shots popped into the bent metal. Raven fired back. He had no solid targets to place his sights on; the bikers had the darkness of the garage to conceal them. But random shots weren't going to hurt.

The enemy stopped shooting. Raven looked ahead for better cover. He wanted to get closer. He ran toward the garage, staying close to the wrecks on his left, firing as he ran, the .45 locking open over the empty magazines. He dived left, rolling, coming up behind another car. He swapped the empty mag for a full one. He was less than 15 yards from the garage.

An engine rumbled and bright halogen lights forced Raven to cover his eyes. The big Mercedes growled as the driver accelerated out of the garage.

Raven fired at the Mercedes. It passed him. He ran after the car and fired again. The Mercedes reached the street and the tires screeched as the driver made a left turn. Another vehicle, an SUV, skidded to a stop while Raven picked up the motorcycle he arrived on. The Raiders called to him from the SUV. Raven dropped the bike and ran to them. Roger opened the back door and Raven jumped inside.

"We going after them?" Darbo said.

"I've risked our necks enough," Raven said. "Get us out of here. We'll deal with the rubbish later."

Darbo hit the accelerator. Raven looked out the back window. Their former not-so-safe house continued to burn. The flames glowed against the night sky. He hoped the fire department arrived soon.

Raven faced forward again and called for their attention.

He related what Clark Wilson had reported moments before the attack took place.

"If they're monitoring cell calls and scanning for your voice," Roger said, "it means they're doing the same for the Weigels."

"Correct, Roger. Which is why I'll need one of you to call Erika. I better stay off the phone for a while."

Darbo said, "This Kohlberg guy knows all the tricks."

"I still have a few," Raven said, "and we'll teach him a thing or two right before I turn out his lights for good."

"I love it when you talk dirty, darling," Lia said with a gleam in her eye. Darbo laughed.

Raven and Roger did not.

Raven was thinking about Erika. He hoped she was okay.

32

Oliver Kohlberg felt a begrudging respect for Sam Raven. He wished they were on the same side. He said so to Hanno.

"Twice he's beaten people we were told were good enough to take him out," he added.

Kohlberg and Hanno sat in the conference room. Hanno activated the screens on the wall; they were five minutes from a meeting with the rest of the Fraternity.

"Raven and his team may not be dead," Hanno pointed out, "but they've also made no progress against us."

"He'll go after Price next."

"He has to *find* Carl first," Hanno said. "Won't matter in 24 hours when the first attack starts. Price will be on the move, and Raven will never catch up. No matter how smart he thinks he is."

When the meeting began, Kohlberg stood and addressed the screens. Bright, high-resolution faces looked back at him. He left out the Raven problem. Instead, Kohlberg explained all assets had moved into place. He advised his members to stay home over the next few days, and especially avoid media attention. The last part was important. They were all men who, by the nature of their business and relationships with the public, were magnets for journalists who wanted their thoughts on record. Kohlberg wanted them to avoid any accidental slips which might give authorities a reason to investigate.

Arthur Hunt and Emma Bell occupied two upper row screens, but Kohlberg ignored them. He'd speak to both privately if he had anything to say, but he felt content, for the moment, in letting Hanno handle them.

"All we have to do now," Kohlberg added, as he began to wrap up the meeting, "is watch the Americans tear themselves apart."

The Fraternity's French representative, a dark-haired man in the middle of the bottom row of monitors, asked, "Where will our people strike first?"

Kohlberg considered the answer a moment. None of his associates knew *all* there was to know about the operation, which was why Weigel couldn't provide Raven with more than the basic idea, and why Raven now sat behind the eight ball without realizing his handicap.

"First strike is Washington, DC," Kohlberg finally said. "After that, like a cracked windshield, our forces will spread and leave onto destruction in their wake."

The old man smiled.

RAVEN and his team made it out of Berlin-Brandenburg without incident. As soon as the Cessna Citation jet reached cruising altitude, Raven asked Darbo to call Erika for an update. The call didn't last long, and Darbo reported all was well and they remained safe and secure.

"Proverbial 'undisclosed location', boss," the big Armenian added.

"That joke is over 20 years old and wasn't funny when it was new," Raven said.

"Well, she wanted to know why you weren't the one calling."

"You explained it well without alarming her, I'd say," Raven replied.

"Nuts. I think they'll move soon just because."

"Not a bad thing."

"I guess. Anybody else you want me to call?"

"Oscar. Tell him I need a trace on a woman named Taylinn Price."

"Got it. Whoa. Is she related to—"

"His ex-wife."

"Oh, this'll be good."

"This isn't a soap opera, but you're free to treat it as such," Raven said.

"She's his ex for maybe the same reason you hate Price?"

"She and I had an affair. Price tried to kill me after."

Lia piped up. "Now *that's* a juicy soap opera. Tell us more."

"Their marriage was rocky enough already. I didn't help but was certainly not the sole contributor. And now you know why Price hates *me*."

Darbo said, "Remind me to keep you away from my women, boss," and called Oscar Morey on Raven's behalf.

CARL PRICE WOKE up in his hotel room and stretched. He had wanted to stay with Emma, but there was too much to do—namely, getting the hell out of Washington, DC. He stayed in bed a little longer anyway because he enjoyed the quiet. He had no idea when he'd be in a peaceful environment again. He had no idea when he'd see Emma again.

Today was the day. Zero hour approached.

He'd be well away from Washington when the first two attacks took place. The distance was important. Once the action began, federal authorities would begin crawling over each scene; he didn't need one to recognize him if he stayed in town. Plus, some members of the other cells might require encouragement in case they felt a chill in their toes. He wanted to keep them properly motivated.

Price felt no doubt about the chain reaction he had put in motion. The re-set the United States was about to go through was long deserved.

He showered, shaved, and grabbed breakfast from the restaurant buffet. Check out at noon, and he was on the road. No last-minute comms with the DC cell; instructions were clear. They knew what to do.

The first of the two DC cells struck at fifteen minutes after noon.

They chose a hamburger stand at a busy shopping center. The stand faced a street packed with lunchtime traffic.

The cell had a two-prong plan. A bomb to blow up the burger stand. Then some automatic rifle fire into any survivors. It had to appear organized, not simply another random mass shooting on the street.

A member of the cell sat at an outdoor table, sorted through her purse with growing alarm, and quickly departed. She had tucked a package under the table before leaving. Nobody in line noticed. The bomb was on a timer, the gun crew standing by in a van about twenty yards away in the shopping center parking lot. The bomb blast sent chunks of the table under which it had been placed into the line of diners, ripping open bodies as the pieces turned into deadly missiles. The shack took part of the explosion, too, two walls crumbling. The follow-up blast from the kitchen's cooking equipment contributed to the oily black plume which climbed skyward. The plume announced disaster to every witness within sight.

The gun crew jumped from the van. They stayed in a half-circle around the vehicle. Targets were plenty, people running, screaming, some taking cover. The automatic rifles chattered and cut down more bodies. The screams almost drowned out the gunfire, and when the gun crew exhausted their magazines, they jumped back into the van for their getaway.

And it was only the beginning...

33

AT CIA HEADQUARTERS, CLARK WILSON WATCHED A CORNER television as the second DC attack took place.

Wilson and Christopher Fisher, the Deputy Director of Operations, sat in the DDO's office discussing the first attack, and the information delivered by Sam Raven. Coverage of the first attack was interrupted by the TV station switching to the second attack, as it happened. The second followed the same pattern as the first.

"All right," Fisher said. He leaned back in his office chair, legs crossed. "No doubt, Raven wasn't wrong."

Wilson sat with his heart racing while Fisher, the longer-serving of the two, remained stoic, his reaction hidden behind a tough poker face.

"This is the kind of attack we are most vulnerable to," Fisher continued. "Cells operating on their own, already in the country. We're not talking about foreign nationals or terrorist suspects of the usual sort. These are Americans organized by somebody on the outside and let loose. If Raven had provided hard data to work with—"

204 | BRIAN DRAKE

Fisher finally broke the mask with a flash of anger. With his jaw tight he switched off the television in disgust.

"We have laws in this country," Fisher said, "which makes stopping this harder than it should be."

"And yet I wouldn't want those laws repealed, either," Wilson said. "Catch-22 for sure."

"Raven was right, and we're in for a world of shit if he can't track down Carl Price. We need him to tie-in Oliver Kohlberg, and maybe this Weigel fellow can provide the testimony. Give Raven whatever he needs or wants. I'll clear it with the DCI."

Wilson left the chair. He wanted to reach Raven right away.

———

CARL PRICE DIDN'T STOP DRIVING all day. He listened to the attack reports on the radio, and hoped the other cells took inspiration from the opening salvo. Attacks were planned in random locations throughout the country until they reached the Rockies. Cells on the West Coast would strike three times a day, and not only in the major cities. They wanted the population living in total panic, with the governmental infrastructure crumbling, within a week.

But the plan wasn't top of mind as he drove. He turned off the radio to better sort his thoughts.

He kept thinking about Sam Raven.

Price knew about the situation in Germany, Raven's failed raid on Kohlberg's house. Raven wasn't going to stop there and he'd shift his attention to catching *him* to gather the intel he needed to defeat the sleeper cells. Price had one area of vulnerability for Raven to exploit, and the more he thought about it, the more Price realized he had to cancel his current course and correct to New York City.

Where Raven could find Price's ex-wife.

Price looked at the dashboard clock. Another two hours till he'd feel safe enough to stop. He'd contact Kohlberg and advise him of the change then. They had to do something about Taylinn before Raven reached her.

Too bad for Tay.

MORE VIOLENT INCIDENTS took place over the next few hours following the DC strikes. Television networks and their "breaking news" elements couldn't keep up. Once the federal government declared the incidents a bona fide terrorist attack in progress, cities around the country set nighttime curfews

In New York City, Chicago, Los Angeles and other major cities the curfews inspired looters. By midnight in each city, major fires burned and emergency crews failed to keep up with frantic 911 calls from frightened residents.

Day One closed with the desired effect. Americans' nerves frayed quickly, and the President's first address to the nation was a smattering of bumper sticker slogans about perseverance and justice. When more attacks began on Day Two, the President vacated DC for Camp David in what critics immediately called a retreat from the front. Americans needed to see their leader at the head of the line and fighting.

The Kohlberg cells continued their violence in New York City.

But this time, Sam Raven was there.

TAYLINN PRICE LEFT her office on Wall Street and 5:30. Her hands shook as she used the key fob to unlock her Audi coupe. She didn't want to admit the crisis had already taken a toll; it had. She'd been in NYC on 9/11. She knew what was happening—again! But she was also a tough New Yorker. It would take more than a bunch of maniacs to send her cowering.

Taylinn was tall and thin with thick red hair. As she eased into the Audi and set a briefcase and purse on the passenger seat, her phone rang. Had the car been on, she'd have talked through the Bluetooth. But she had to hold the phone to answer, which she did with a curt, "Hello?"

"Hey, it's Berta. You still going?"

Roberta Simmons worked as a market analyst at Taylinn's previous job. They'd become best friends during Taylinn's time there, unlike several other "Friends" Tay might name.

"I am if you are."

"I'm not sure."

"Come on. I'll buy you a glass of wine."

"Has anybody else backed out?" Berta said.

"No, we're a united front. Safety in numbers. We'll be all right as long as we're home by ten."

"Gawd, it's like I'm 15 again. *Curfews?* I swear we have nothing but idiots in charge."

"So I'll see you at the restaurant?"

Berta sighed. "Yeah, I'll be there. But if it gets crazy, I'm outta there."

"Fair enough." Taylinn said good-bye and ended the call. She drove out of the garage and into thick city traffic. She wasn't the only one going about her life, damn the torpedoes. Cabs and buses choked lanes. Cars barely moved. The usual sounds tried to break through the Audi's cocoon, horns, yells, chugging bus engines. It gave Taylinn a welcome sense of normalcy. Presently traffic moved forward. A bus passed her with a movie ad on one side. It was a comedy advertised as the featured star's "triumphant" return to the silver screen. Taylinn already had plans to stay home opening night.

The left lanes where the bus traveled started to move better than the right lane where Taylinn remained stuck. She watched it travel partway through the intersection.

A bright flash within the bus's interior turned the windows from front to back into deadly glass shards propelled by an orange fireball. The shockwave forced the two cars ahead of Taylinn back into her Audi; the crunch of metal, jolt of the impact, and collision with the car behind her took seconds, and Taylinn's scream drowned out the other noises.

Out! Get out!

34

HER HANDS CLAWED FOR THE SEATBELT. SCREAMS ECHOED around her. She wasn't cognizant of anything not happening within the Audi. Then she froze because new sounds joined the fray. A sound she had never wanted to hear again after her marriage ended.

The rapid *pop pop pop* meant nothing other than automatic gunfire. Taylinn twisted around in her seat. People ran from their cars; bodies fell. She snapped off her seatbelt and bolted from the car with her purse, tripping and falling painfully to her knees. She shouldn't have worn a skirt. One couldn't properly run for one's life in a skirt with a tight hem. But the fall saved her from the line of auto fire aimed at her car. Bullets rocked the metal and punctured windows. Taylinn hit the grimy asphalt as the hail passed over. She jumped up and ran as best as the hem of her skirt and heels allowed. Her vision spun, darkened slightly; she wanted to get to the sidewalk. The closest sidewalk, on her right. She might find refuge in an alley if a bullet didn't find her back first.

People ran and screamed; somebody jostled her and kept

going. Taylinn gained the sidewalk and stole a look behind. Three men with AK rifles—she'd never forget the shape—walked along the line of stopped cars with their weapons held at the hip.

They fired at random, without aim, and flame flashed from the muzzles as they swung from one side to the other.

Taylinn screamed as a powerful arm wrapped around her. Her feet left the ground; bullets smacked the wall where she'd been. Whoever had her, pulled her into an alley. She kicked and struggled but the grip didn't break.

"Taylinn!" a man yelled in her ear. "It's Sam! Sam Raven!"

She stopped struggling and tried to turn her head. The way Raven held her, she had no way to see his face until he let go. He pulled her to the ground behind a pile of stacked pallets.

Taylinn examined the face of the man before her. He was Raven, for sure. The face looked older, but she supposed she did, too.

"Are you hurt?" he said.

"No!" She had to shout as the gunners moved closer to the alley. Raven told her to stay put as he drew a handgun from under his gray sports jacket. He dashed to the mouth of the alley with the gun in a two-hand grip. She watched him shoot. He fired—once, twice. The loud pistol kicked with each shot. The brick near his face exploded in tiny shards as a bullet struck; he flinched, shifted his stance, and fired again and again. Spent brass bounced on the sidewalk at his feet. More empty shells fell as he emptied the magazine and then slapped in a re-load.

He extended the gun again, but didn't fire. Taylinn heard no more gunfire in reply. She only heard people still screaming.

Raven put his gun away and returned to her. She slung her purse cross-body and took his hand and followed as he ran to the opposite end of the alley, where they met another man Raven introduced as Darbo. The other man smiled at her.

"We gotta keep moving," Raven said. They joined the flow of people fleeing the area on foot. Vehicles remained stopped in the street. Darbo said somebody named Lia was parked a block over and Raven told him to lead the way.

RAVEN HELPED Taylinn into the van driven by Lia. Traffic a few blocks from the explosion moved a little better, and Lia was able to merge into the flow to get them away from the carnage. Raven felt the heat of the Nighthawk .45 under his arm. It was still hot from firing.

Darbo moved to the third-row seat to watch out the back window. Raven and Taylinn occupied the middle.

Taylinn's face was flush with heat; she wiped sweat from her face. She might be frightened but she wasn't hysterical—the old days of dealing with her ex hadn't departed entirely. She still knew how to keep together under stress.

"What's going on?" she said.

"Fair question."

"You got a fair answer? And why are you in the same place as me?"

"It involves Carl."

"Oh my *God*, really? What now?"

Raven took his time explaining the situation. Taylinn listened, she didn't interrupt, but the expression on her face turned from curiosity to shock, surprise, and then doubt.

"You're nuts," she told Raven. "This is absolutely the craziest thing I've ever heard, and I live in New York City."

Lia laughed.

"The bus blowing up was real," Raven said. "Those bullets were real."

"Okay, okay. You're right. But still—it's insane."

"And we need your help to stop the insanity."

"I can't believe you're saying that to me."

"Taylinn—"

"You and Carl have never changed. He's out raising hell for who knows what, probably nothing more than money, and you sweep in and play the white knight. You're both going to end up dead somewhere and I really hope I'm not around to see it."

Raven grinned. "Another woman said the same thing the other day."

"You should pay attention to the women in your life and get out while you're ahead."

"You know I can't."

She let out a breath. "I know. What do you want from me?"

"Can you help us find Carl?"

"No. I have no clue where he is. Sometimes he gets drunk and calls me begging me to take him back. Will his number help?"

"Yes, it will."

Raven wondered if it was the break he'd been waiting for. He sat back and let Lia drive the van.

LIA DROVE across the bridge to Manhattan where the curfew rush had ended and only a few vehicles drove with them. Taylinn directed Lia to her condo and handed her the key card to access the underground garage. She told Lia to park in her assigned space.

Darbo, still at the back window, used his cell to call Roger

Justice and tell him they'd arrived. Roger already had Taylinn's condo secured. When she became upset over the break-in, Raven told her she needed better security. Her resulting glare suggested she didn't hold any warm feelings whatsoever regarding his reply. Raven knew she'd agree after she had time to think it over.

———————

TAYLINN WANTED to know what the four of them expected to do now that they were in her condo.

Raven answered.

"Give us Carl's number, assuming he didn't change it, and then we'll get you someplace safe."

"Where?"

"Out of New York."

"Somewhere safe outside of New York? Are you watching the news, Sam? Paying any attention at all? You can't go anywhere without buses blowing up ten feet away from you!"

Raven checked the first reply that came to mind. Maybe he was wrong about how she was reacting to the crisis; maybe she couldn't handle combat the way she once had.

"But, fine, whatever," she concluded, sorting through her purse for her phone. She tossed the device to Raven. "Look it up. "It's under J for Jerk Ex Husband I Never Want to See Again."

Raven remained quiet and scrolled through her contact list while she stewed. He felt the presence of Lia, Roger, and Darbo behind him. They'd elected to keep quiet, too. Raven knew how to pick smart people.

The best bet for Taylinn *was* to get her out of NYC. A safe place might be a rural one, where Kohlberg's forces wouldn't show. It made no sense to bomb Mayberry when blowing up Chicago made for better headlines and pictures.

He'd ask Lia to escort her somewhere. The Russian fireball would give him hell for taking her out of the fight.

Raven found Carl Price's number and passed the phone to Roger Justice. Roger took the phone to a laptop he'd placed on the dining table. Two boxes with flashing lights were connected to the laptop, the functions of which Raven didn't understand, and he decided not to waste time asking about. Roger sat and placed the phone on one of the boxes and began typing commands.

Taylinn said, "I guess you can all sit down if you want. Who wants a glass of wine?"

Raven thought she certainly needed one.

35

CARL PRICE CROSSED INTO A DEAD NEW YORK CITY WITH A quarter tank of gas and hate in his heart. Kohlberg had told him no. He refused to re-direct cell units to deal with his ex-wife, who, the old man said, may not even be a problem. Price knew Kohlberg was wrong, but didn't tell him why. *She's a threat because now and then I get drunk and call her.*

Manhattan. He had to reach the bridge to get to Taylinn's condo. He drove fast, blowing through intersections, grinning at the ghost town feel of the city.

Police cherry lights flashed in his rearview mirror.

Price cursed and beat on the steering wheel. He slowed and pulled over and unzipped his jacket to allow easy access to the FN-FNX .45-cal autoloader under his right arm. He'd loaded the gun with armor-piercing cartridges. The cops would never know what hit them.

The two patrolmen approached the car on either side.

Price drew the FN pistol.

He rolled down his window and the cop on his side managed to say, "You better have a good reason—" before the FN .45 barked once. The bullet punched through the cop's vest; he fell back as Price opened the door and rolled onto the street. The second cop had his gun out, and was coming around the back to fire as he yelled into his radio. Price fired rapidly, the cop's words choking off. He looked surprised. His vest was supposed to stop this sort of thing from happening. By the time he hit the pavement, he wasn't thinking anymore.

Price left them both bleeding out on the street, but aware he now had a new problem.

He had to ditch the car. The cops had called in the stop.

Well, he had an idea for how to solve the problem.

———

ROGER JUSTICE ANNOUNCED he had a ping on Carl Price's phone.

"Where?" Raven leaned over Roger's shoulder.

"Here in New York. It's within this circled area."

"A hair outside Manhattan."

"He's here?" Taylinn jumped from up from the couch. A look from Raven stopped her halfway to him.

"We need to get you away from here," Raven said. "Lia, can you manage?"

"A little sleep will be nice first," the Russian woman said from the couch. She sipped her wine. Raven had seen her down two glasses already.

He checked his watch. It was getting late indeed, and he didn't want to risk the women being on the road in the middle of the city's curfew.

"All right," he said, "leave first thing in the morning. Let's all try and rest. I'll take the first watch and then Roger, then Darbo. Lia gets to sleep."

Lia held up her wine glass. "Yay!"

"What are you afraid of, Sam?" Taylinn said.

"Carl's only here for one reason. He knows I'll be looking for you."

"So he's—"

"Come to kill you."

"Oh," she said.

CARL PRICE DITCHED his car in a parking garage and walked the rest of the way, keeping to the dark alleys and shadow-enveloped alcoves. He wanted to avoid any further entanglements with police. He only had to go two blocks, but hunkered down in alleys along the way to watch the empty streets and dark storefronts for threats. The silence of the city gave him an eerie feeling. Cities were supposed to be noisy, hubs of life and activity. The sad part was the curfew made no difference. There were still areas of rioting, but not on the same scale as Day One, and no activity where Price was now.

The red-green-yellow glow of a traffic light rotated as designed, a slight clicking noise coming from the box each time the light changed. It always made the noise, he reflected, but nobody ever heard it. The colors combated with the glow of the streetlamps lining the road.

The glow almost disguised the flashing lights of an approaching police cruiser. Price waited for the patrol car to pass. It went by at a higher speed than normal. Price figured the bodies of the two cops he'd shot had been found by now, and the department was on high alert. He had to watch his step.

Stay put; there may be more.

Price remained in place for ten more minutes, then felt safe enough to move. He left the alley and continued his advance. Not much farther to go, but the blocks in NYC were long ones. It took another forty minutes of his start-and-stop pattern to reach a closed bar called The Horsehead. He tapped a hurried code on the door, but didn't get an answer right away. He tapped the code again. Nothing. He stayed in the shadow of the doorway and cursed inwardly. Where were they? He tapped the code again.

Finally, the lock clicked back.

"It's Price. Let me in."

He didn't see the face of the person behind the door.

"You're not supposed to be here," said the man opposite the door.

"Emergency. Open the door."

The door squeaked open and Price slipped inside. The door shut behind him. He turned to see the man holding a pistol.

"You know me," Price said. "Put the piece away or I'll make you eat it."

Low light from the bar gave the seating area a glow. Price saw the man's face. His name was Holden. The man obeyed the command and said, "Sorry. Surely you understand."

"Of course."

"What's the emergency?"

"I need a rifle, ammo and a car."

"This isn't part of our instructions."

Price closed the gap between him and Holden in a flash. Price jammed the muzzle of the FN .45 into Holden's gut. The other man sucked in a sharp breath.

"I said, 'Emergency.' Are you deaf?"

Holden swallowed. "Okay. Come below."

Price put away his gun and followed Holden through the maze of tables to a rear door. Steps on the other side led to a basement, and Holden switched on a light.

Holden was the same height as Price, and walked with tiredness.

"Aren't you sleeping?" Price said.

"Could you?"

Price didn't answer. They reached the bottom and Holden used a key to unlock another door. They stepped through. Four members of the Manhattan team sat around. They looked whipped. Price frowned. There should have been three more.

"Where are the rest?"

Holden faced him. "Dead."

"Cops?"

"No. Somebody else."

Raven.

It made sense Sam Raven had arrived before him, but Price had hoped for a little more time.

"Then I *really* need what I asked for," the former CIA man said.

36

ALL RAVEN HAD TO DO WAS MAKE SURE THE CURTAINS STAYED closed, but he knew better than to leave the safety of Taylinn to curtains. Roger had easily defeated Taylinn's security system, after all. Price wouldn't have a hard time at all if he really tried.

And Price would likely come down from the roof. They were too high up to make an effective assault from the ground floor. A little fast-roping from the top and an assault team could land on the balcony and crash through. Raven had his pistol and the well-worn HK416 with which to fight until the others joined in, should something happen, but for now he felt they were okay.

His phone rang. Raven looked at the caller ID. Clark Wilson again. He answered.

"Clark?"

"You out of Germany?"

"Yes, we're in New York City. What's happening?"

"Everything you're seeing there is times ten across the country. All hell's breaking loose and we can't keep up."

"Tell me more."

"Local cops and the FBI are simply overwhelmed. We're dealing with multiple strikes a day, as you know, sometimes in the same city, and by the time they set up at one crime scene, another pops up. Evidence is being lost, bad guys are getting away, the whole bit. There's captured cell phone footage, but the attackers cover their faces well."

"What about on your end?" Raven said.

"There's no overseas connection we can confirm at this point."

"Goddammit, Clark, I *gave* you one."

"But we're going on your *word*, Sam. We need hard data. Evidence. *Testimony*. We need to talk to the Weigels."

"I'm not bringing Philip Weigel to you until I know your end is secure. Can you assure me there are no leaks after what happened in Berlin?"

"We're still working on it."

"We don't have a lot of time. How about a Zoom?"

Wilson laughed. "Fine. See if you can get them to agree."

"If it helps, I'm close to Price."

"How close?"

"Remember Taylinn?"

"Oh, God, Sam, be careful."

"Once I get her out of here, we're making moves."

"You have a zero on Price?"

"He's here, too. For her. He had the same idea as me."

Wilson sighed. "Kohlberg had this plan ready to go for years, didn't he?"

"According to Weigel, yes."

"Is he safe?"

"His daughter is taking care of them."

"We need a statement from him to convince the top of Kohlberg's involvement. It's the only way, but even if Weigel gives us everything, the wheels turn slowly."

"Kohlberg is counting on that. We have rules. The rules fail in a situation such as this."

"Take Price alive if you can."

"You forget I'm not beholden to the rules, Clark. Not *these* rules. If there's anything left for you to collect once the smoke clears, I'll bring you a souvenir."

MORNING CAME, finally, and they made plans over breakfast. Lia would drive Taylinn out of the city while Raven, Darbo and Roger took care of Price. Roger pinpointed Price's location to a bar across the city; Raven figured the tavern was the hideout of the Kohlberg cell. Price had come in without the weapons he needed, and the cell had them. He wasn't there any longer, but they had the address.

A sense of relief fell over Raven once he watched Lia and Taylinn drive away in the van. Taylinn was out of danger. Now he and Roger and Darbo had nothing to hold them back.

The bar was still closed as they paid their first visit. Raven didn't know who owned the Horsehead, but he had a feeling the fellow was as tied to Kohlberg as Weigel. Why else would he host a kill squad? The other question was *how* they used the bar as a base of operations. What coordination, if any, did they have with other cells? Or were they all acting on their own without communicating with the others? Had it been Raven's operation, no cell would know *anything* about another. He knew Kohlberg's mindset had to be similar. If not, Price had made the suggestion. Raven knew how Price thought, too.

Raven wanted to know the layout of the bar. They needed to know what they were working with inside. Back at Taylinn's condo, Roger went to work researching the information. Floorplan, blueprints, whatever. The documentation wasn't hard to obtain.

DARBO KEPT HIS VOICE LOW. "Don't you wish we could bust in and shoot the hell out of the place and call it a day?"

"Not yet. I'd like to know *exactly* what I'm shooting the hell out *of* before doing so."

It was never a second thought to Raven. Too many reasons not to—the wave of pedestrians, the traffic—sat in the line of fire, and none of them had a clue. Raven's second rule, no gunfights in public, was there to make sure they remained in the dark.

The bar didn't open till noon; they watched for over an hour until a tall man with shaggy white hair unlocked the doors and entered. Darbo snapped his picture. "Not sure I got a good angle."

"We'll try and ID him anyway," Raven said.

They returned to the condo where Roger had good news.

"Here's the design specs for the bar. Normal layout till right here. It's a stairway behind a door between the restrooms. It leads to this basement which is probably a storeroom."

"A very large storeroom," Raven noted. "Large enough for a few bad guys to hide out."

Darbo took out his cell. "Can we see if my pic of the owner is any good?"

Roger plugged the cell phone into the laptop via Darbo's charging cable. Roger dropped the side-profile picture of the white-haired man into an ID scanning program.

"The profile might hurt," Roger said.

"I thought so."

The computer beeped.

"Nope, we got lucky," Roger said.

A mugshot popped up on the right side of the monitor with the cell pic on the left.

"David Mark Graves," Roger said. "Age 65. Long rap sheet, as you can see. Lots of arrests for various protests around the country. Perhaps that's how he landed on Kohlberg's radar."

"One of the true believers," Raven said.

"He's been raging against the machine his whole life?" Darbo chuckled.

"Until the left-wing socio-fascist movement became the machine," Raven said.

"What do we do with him?" Darbo said. He looked at Raven, who began to pace with his arms folded.

"Do we have an address for this paragon of virtue?" Raven asked without looking at either Roger or Darbo.

"Yup."

Raven stopped. "Then we go see him tonight. We need the keys to the bar, after all."

37

LIA KENISOVA APPRECIATED THAT TAYLINN HADN'T ARGUED TO try and stay.

Neither spoke as Lia drove the van. The Russian woman occasionally glanced at Taylinn in the passenger seat, but the other woman's face remained blank, her stare set forward with her eyes taking in nothing in particular.

Lia had the feeling that no matter what Taylinn had experienced in the past, the current situation had taxed her reserve. She might have considered Price part of her past, but now he'd come roaring back with violence, and the target on her back wasn't only Raven's imagination. The question nobody asked was if Price would have come after his wife had Raven not been involved, but it was moot. Raven and Price clashed early in the conflict, and set the chain reaction in motion.

Lia felt the responsibility to make sure the chain reaction didn't end in a flame out resulting in Taylinn's demise. Or hers.

Lia kept driving and didn't bother to try and fill the

silence. Taylinn needed space; Lia would let her have it, and let Taylinn break the silence when she wanted.

ROGER JUSTICE YELLED FOR RAVEN.

Raven left the kitchen and hurried to the dining table where Roger still sat. His laptop monitor showed a digital outline of the city.

"What's wrong?"

"Price's cell phone. I just did another check and there's no trace of him."

"Did he switch it off?"

"I'd still get something. More likely he destroyed it."

Darbo wandered over but didn't add anything to the conversation.

Raven's phone rang. He reached for it and glanced at the screen. "It's Lia." He answered and said, "Everything all right?"

The voice he heard in reply did not belong to Lia.

"Hello, Sam."

"Price."

"We didn't get to talk last time we saw each other. How you been?"

"What have you done, Carl?"

"I have your woman and my ex-wife. Nice try getting them out of here. I tracked them the same way you were probably tracking me."

"Your fight is with *me*, not them."

"I have a few things to settle with Taylinn, don't worry. Here is what I propose. You wait by the phone and I will send our location. You will come alone. If I see the other two clowns with you, your woman and my ex both die and you'll never see me again."

"Oh, I'll see you, Carl. Bet on it."

"There is no time for bravado, Sam. Wait for my text."

"Let me talk to Lia."

"She can't come to the phone. Her head is bashed in a bit. She's sleeping it off."

Raven grasped the phone tight, clenching his jaw. Rage filled him. "Let me talk to Taylinn."

"No." Price disconnected. Raven dropped his phone on the table and looked around for something to kick. But he steadied himself after a moment and faced the quiet stares of Roger and Darbo.

"Do I have to repeat?"

"We got it, boss," said Darbo.

"All right. Change of plans…"

THEY HAD to hustle before curfew hit and the cops swept any stragglers off the street. The NYPD made no secret if they caught anybody after the appointed time, they'd spend the night in a cell. If they found the automatic rifle in Raven's car, his one-nighter would turn into an all-lifer. It was an issue they needed specifically to avoid, and Price banked on the difficulty by sending Raven an address in Montauk, Long Island. Roger checked the distance. Three hours away.

By car, anyway. Raven wished either Roger or Darbo knew how to fly, or one of them had easy access to a chopper. He'd have to drive and he needed to start right away.

Price wanted to meet at midnight, at the shore, at the lighthouse on Montauk Point. They'd have to skip the Horsehead Bar, but Raven hadn't forgotten about the owner. He passed the name to Clark shortly before his departure. Let the Feds handle him, Raven decided. The mission was coming to a close, and fast, with the one thing Raven wanted to avoid—the loss of innocent life—on the line. He wasn't only thinking about the public targeted by Kohlberg's forces. Taylinn Price was also looking down the barrel at death, and Raven had to keep the worst from happening to her. She wasn't supposed to have been hurt.

Raven drove with his hands tight on the steering wheel, cursing himself for ever coming near New York City, trying to find other ways he might have tracked down Carl Price without involving his ex-wife. Alternate ideas did not come to mind. She'd been the only option from the beginning, the only way to search for the man Raven knew had every detail of the Kohlberg plan trapped within his head.

He needed Price alive.

As much as he disliked the thought, he needed Price in one piece.

Best laid plans and all that. Raven knew the "plan" he and Darbo and Roger hastily assembled wouldn't last longer than it took for the first bullet to fly.

He hoped Roger and Darbo were somewhere behind him. Nothing showed in the rearview mirror but darkness. He was the only one on the road.

Two hours, fifty-nine minutes. Raven felt tired from the drive. He stopped once for gas at the midway point, and the station's shop had been closed. Luckily his debit card worked at the pump.

He paid little attention to Montauk as he drove through town. He followed Highway 27—Montauk Highway—and his destination lay at the literal end of the road. The Montauk Lighthouse sat on a point of land jutting into the North Atlantic. He figured Price had recruited the remaining cell members from the Horsehead Bar, and hoped Roger and Darbo remained discreet in their approach. Price and his people would be watching, and for all Raven knew he'd passed several observation points already, assuming the opposition knew what car he was using. Raven didn't want to give Price too much credit, but also knew not giving him *any* was unwise.

Raven switched his headlamps to bright when he left the town limit. The city lights shined in the rearview, but ahead was all black, forest on either side. He was on the last stretch of Highway 27 before he reached the lighthouse. And still, nobody behind him. Had Darbo and Roger broken down? Stopped by police? Raven took a deep breath. He had to be ready to face Price alone indeed.

He had his Nighthawk pistol, the HK rifle, combat vest, and a backup gun hidden in an ankle holster on his right leg. The backup had been Darbo's idea, and the big Armenian provided both gun and holster. Raven wasn't entirely familiar with Darbo's Glock G36, but the compact gun was chambered in .45 ACP like the Nighthawk Custom and Raven knew Glocks were easy to handle. He hoped the need didn't arise. If he was going for a hideout piece, he'd be in bad trouble for sure. Best case, he had the Glock to give to Lia.

His headlights flashed on a sign announcing the light-house ahead.

38

THE ROADWAY CURVED LEFT AS HIGHWAY 27 LOOPED AROUND two large oval parking areas. The lighthouse, the strobe in the glass top at the tip sending its rotating beam into the ocean, stood like a lone sentry. Raven tried to see more in the beam of his headlamps as he turned into one of the lots, but he found no indication Price, Lia and Taylinn, or any other gunners had arrived ahead of him.

Raven wasn't so early as to think he'd beat them; Price would have made sure he was in position well before Raven showed up.

He shut off the car.

He parked with a tree line behind him, and left the car, grabbing his rifle and combat vest, to take cover in the trees and survey some more. The openness didn't help either. The parking ovals were wide open; so was the lighthouse, stone paths through trimmed grass leading to the structure at the far point. The North Atlantic might as well have been a black curtain made of velvet. Raven saw nothing beyond the shore, but he heard the waves. What normally would have brought a sense of calm and peace to a troubled mind now only hid the movement of a concealed enemy intent on killing him.

What was he waiting for?

His phone rang. The sudden blast of the ringtone, even at low volume, startled him. He answered.

"I'm here."

"We saw you. I think I know where you're hiding, too," Price said.

"You didn't tell me to stand in the open, Carl."

"But I *am* impressed you followed instructions and came alone."

"You have a friend of mine and somebody who wasn't supposed to get hurt."

Price said, "There's where you fail, Sam. Always. Every time. When you get a civilian involved, bad things happen. How many have you lost already, Sam? Have you learned to ignore the ghosts?"

"What makes you think I can?"

Where the hell are Roger and Darbo?

You're on your own, Sam. Think!

Price laughed, though Raven didn't hear him clearly as waves thundered onto shore.

"You want to get this show on the road, Carl?"

"I'm ready. See the lighthouse?"

"Yes."

"Come on up. Take the steps or the elevator, I don't care which."

"Where are Lia and Taylinn?"

"Close by. If you survive, you deserve to find them, don't worry."

"See you in a minute, old pal."

"I'll be waiting, Sam."

Raven disconnected and dropped the phone at the base of a tree. Worst case, Roger and Darbo could find him by tracing the signal—if the worst happened.

Be he had no intention of dying tonight.

He wanted to show Carl Price the meaning of *payback*.

RAVEN REMAINED in place and examined the tall lighthouse. A building before the tower was a museum; another structure sat on the ocean side behind it. Over the edge, rocks; to the left, a ledge of sand. No way Price waited at the top of the lighthouse. There was not enough room to fight in the glass chamber at the top. They needed more room to groove.

Opposite the second parking lot were more trees and from there he could follow the curving portion of the road to the gate which barred access to the lighthouse road.

Raven donned the combat vest and zipped the front end together, checked the HK, and moved out. He ran fast but not in a straight line. He varied his speed and zigzagged to keep a potential sniper from having a clear shot. But snipers didn't really bother him. He wanted to know where Price was truly hiding. The lighthouse was a ruse to draw Raven into the open. If he'd been pulling the same maneuver, he'd be hiding somewhere close but not easily detected —such as the rocky crescent at the edge of the point. Price and his troops had no comfort if they were waiting there, but it made sense. It almost didn't matter *where* the ambush came from. Raven knew *nobody* waited for him in the lighthouse.

Through the first parking lot, across a patch of brush on a slope; into the second. His shoes scraped on the blacktop but he barely discerned the sound over his pounding pulse and the crash of waves. The wind off the ocean blew cold. The sweat on his face and neck dried quickly.

He reached the road where trees provided more interference. Running across to the shoulder, he rolled into the dirt and stopped on his belly.

Raven jerked his gaze to the right. He'd seen something—a short flash of light, not to be repeated, but it meant Darbo and Roger had arrived. The flash came from the patch of trees near the edge of the first parking lot closest to the highway. They were with him after all, though he knew they had no idea if he saw the signal. But if he'd seen the brief flash, had Price, too?

Raven shook the question away and started forward. He followed the edge of the pavement to Lighthouse Road; it branched off the curved portion of Highway 27 to stop at a gate. The gate wasn't much, a bar to raise and lower, and wasn't very high; there was also room to walk around. Raven did so, staying close to the guard kiosk left of the entryway.

Lighthouse Road continued straight ahead, leading to the museum building and the lighthouse behind. To the left, open grass carved out a portion of forest, the far edge ringed with trees. The waves increased in volume since he was closer than before, but not even the roar of nature drowned out the chatter of automatic weapons fire which began as Raven examined the area.

The first barrage crackled from the grassy area to the left, shooter laying prone in the open. Raven rolled away. He rolled left, getting up to run to another building—the lighthouse visitor's center. The far corner of the structure blocked the prone gunners' aim, but not the sights of whoever opened fire directly behind him.

Raven dropped and rolled again and the incoming gunfire chewed the front of the visitors' center. He crawled across the railed porch. The new set of gunners fired from a storage and maintenance building across the road, less than 100 yards away—too close. Raven fired back, glad to finally have a chance to shoot at the enemy who had caused to much chaos, violence and death.

The HK bucked against his shoulder. He had no visual ID on the shooters' position, so he shifted his aim with each two-round controlled burst. He let off the trigger. No return fire. But only because now he felt more than heard approaching footsteps vibrating through the ground. The first set of gunners were rushing towards the building.

Raven turned to meet them.

39

THE FIRST GUNNER TO APPROACH TRIED TO FIRE AROUND THE corner while limiting his exposure. Raven stroked the trigger of the HK416 and sent a 5.56mm mankiller through the wood, which missed the gunner as it passed through, but the gunner yelled as shards of wood sprayed into his face. He moved—exposing too much. Raven fired twice more and the wet slaps of slugs ripping through clothing and into flesh signaled a good kill. The gunner pitched backward and fell, almost colliding with his buddy who sidestepped and shouldered his weapon.

Raven let another pair of slugs go and watched the second gunner's head snap back. He landed next to his buddy.

Raven ran to the dead men as auto fire resumed from the shed, but none of the rounds touched him as he melted into the shadows around the corner. He slammed a full mag into the HK and dropped to one knee. Time to process his options. The shooting from the shed stopped. They couldn't see him anymore than he saw them.

But the threat remained.

Where was Price hiding?

Not the lighthouse. Then where?

The museum. Or the second building behind the lighthouse.

If he stayed on the grass and moved fast enough, he might avoid the gunners in the shed. He started forward—

And dropped back as gunfire chunked into the side of the building. He dropped prone again.

They had night vision.

They *could* see him.

The shooting paused.

"Great," Raven muttered. "Pinned down."

Another stream of fire erupted at the storage building, but the shooting wasn't confined to the structure. Muzzle flashes winked in a strobe pattern; then silence again

Raven frowned.

Then he grinned. Roger and Darbo had arrived.

He made no signal to them nor they him. They knew he'd understand. Raven left the visitors' center and charged across the grass.

One way or another, it was time to settle accounts with Carl Price once and for all.

RAVEN KICKED open the door to the lighthouse museum and dove right. He went through a doorway to a display room.

The narrow hallway leading front to back wasn't the place to get caught in the open. A stairway led upstairs—the steps adjoined the hall on the left side. Silence, short of Raven's breathing and the muted ocean.

He eased to his feet and left the room to explore. He followed the hall and checked each room along the right side. A solid wall covered the left side to support the stairs. He checked all the way to the back. No sign of life. Upstairs? No. Price wouldn't go where he only had one way out. He wasn't the type to dive out a window, which was sure suicide anyway since the only way to go was down to the hard earth.

Raven exited out the back door. The glare of the lighthouse lit the area for a brief moment.

A pistol cracked. The doorway on Raven's right exploded into pieces. Raven yelled as debris stabbed his skin. He bent and rolled onto the ground.

"You didn't listen, Sam!"

Price! Raven tried to find him in the dark. No dice. The lighthouse flashed its beacon again. There! Standing on the grass away from the building behind the tower. He held a gun and—

A detonator.

Raven pulled the HK into firing position.

The light went out.

Raven fired into the dark.

The building behind the lighthouse exploded in a flash of orange fire, the wooden building collapsing like a house of cards as fire ate and snapped at the remains.

No! Were the women inside? If so—

He'd lost both Lia and Taylinn.

With a scream, Raven ran into the dark. The lighthouse flashed. In the moment of light, Raven saw Price running at him. Two irresistible forces about to collide—

Raven hit Price low in the chest, striking with the butt-stock of the HK, driving the wind out of him, knocking the pistol from Price's grasp. The blow didn't stop Price's forward momentum. He pushed Raven back and off balance, and both men fell like trees with Price on top.

Raven held the HK between them, a hand on either end, and he pushed Price off with a yell of exertion. Rolling left as he did so, Price tumbled away. Both jumped to their feet and squared off, Raven bringing the HK to bear. The glow of the fire lit the area; shadows flickered; Raven zeroed his sights.

Price grabbed the barrel and pulled Raven to him, slamming a fist into Raven's face, following with a kick to his midsection. Raven doubled over and Price pulled at the HK, freeing the rifle from Raven's grasp, but unable to get the sling off his arm. Raven grasped at the trigger to shoot Price in the belly. Price instead shoved the buttstock into Raven's chin.

Raven's head snapped back and his vision spun. He started to fall but something held him upright. The sling! Price used a knife and sliced the strap. The sling released and Raven landed on his back. Price shuffled away with the HK and laughed as he took aim.

Raven rolled, reaching for his pistol, Price's shots tearing into the grass. Raven extended the Nighthawk .45 and fired once. The back of Price's head exploded with chunks of skull and brain but the hole in his forehead appeared small. Raven watched Price's body fall and climbed to his feet. He turned to the flaming mass behind the lighthouse. Smoke stung his eyes and made him choke. Nothing inside could have survived. If he tried to get close, he'd only succumb to the heat and smoke.

He'd failed to rescue Lia and Taylinn and take Price alive, but as he stowed his gun and looked down at his former friend's body, he wondered if he might still find a clue to prevent the mission from becoming a total failure.

First, he grabbed the HK416, then knelt beside Price's body. It only took a moment to find Price's cell phone and he dropped it into a pocket. More smoke blew in his direction. He had to find Darbo and Roger and get away. There'd be time to mourn their losses later. Escaping was the priority now.

40

"SAM!"

Raven pivoted toward the sound of his name. Both Darbo and Roger waved him in their direction, and they each carried something—no, *somebody*. Darbo held Lia, Roger grasped Taylinn; both women remained semi-bound and barely walked on their own, but their hands were free. Raven ran to them.

"They got out," Roger reported, as they breathed hard, "when he left to confront you."

"Let's get 'em out of here," Raven said.

"What about the curfew?"

Raven wasn't sure what to do about the curfew.

Time to get creative...

THEY DROVE a few miles south to Camp Hero, a camp ground near the ocean, and set about taking care of Lia and Taylinn.

Price had roughed up Taylinn a little but she wasn't

injured. Lia had a growing welt on the side of her face where she'd been struck by the barrel of a pistol.

Price and his gun crew, Lia reported, intercepted the van on the way to Connecticut. They'd boxed in the van and shot out the tires; Lia said she had no chance to fight back while trying to keep the van upright.

Lia and Taylinn rested in the car driven by Darbo and Roger. The three men stood near the shore to talk. The fire at the lighthouse cast an orange glow in the sky; emergency crews raced by the camp ground, lights and sirens wailing. Raven hoped they could save the historic lighthouse from suffering too much damage.

"What now?" Roger said.

"We still have the bar man, Graves, to talk to," Raven said. "And this." He produced Price's cell phone. "Think you can manage something with it, Roger?"

Roger took the phone. "Sure. Back at the condo."

"I'm afraid we're sleeping on the beach tonight, gentleman. You two doze in my car. I'll take first watch."

"You sure?" Darbo said. "You look rough. Took a few hits yourself, you know."

Raven shook his head. "I have a lot of thinking to do, Darbo. I'll shake you awake when it's your turn."

The two Raiders said okay, turned and walked away.

Raven faced the ocean, still dark as it stretched to infinity, and inhaled the salt-tinged air. He didn't want to dwell on Price too much. Yes, there had been a conflict between them. A personal battle. But Price had gone bad, too. He'd worked with the enemy to undermine the country he once claimed to defend. Raven had faced many similar cases before—the draw of the dollar was too strong for some. He'd always dismissed them as accidents. But he secretly feared his own turn to "the dark side" should he ever lose sight of his goals, his reason for fighting. He was afraid he wouldn't recognize the change, should it come over him, until it was too late.

All the more reason to never lose sight of what he had to do, never take short cuts in his war without end.

He stood on the sand and stared into space, feeling the chill of the ocean wind, wishing his life had gone another way. But then he touched the lockets dangling beneath his shirt. He could wish, but it wouldn't change anything.

TAYLINN'S CONDO once again became a base of operations once they returned the next morning. They almost used up the hot water taking turns in the shower, but Darbo and Taylinn helped revive worn spirits with a big breakfast.

Raven watched Taylinn eat. He needed to talk to her about last night. He needed to process last night himself.

Nothing was simple or easy. If Raven had a way to disconnect feelings, reactions, emotions, all of what made humans human, he would. No question. Some experiences were too much to deal with, and it was easier not to bother. He wasn't somebody who had the luxury of ignoring what raged inside him, and neither was Taylinn.

They'd talk later; not now.

Roger had the floor.

"What are we looking for on Price's phone?"

"Names," Raven said as he swallowed a bite of pancake. "Recent calls. I want to know who he's communicated with since he arrived back in the US, and their numbers. We need to get everything to Clark at CIA as fast as we can."

Later, the television news showed how desperate the government was to get a handle on the out-of-control violence and law enforcement's inability to contain the chaos. *Some of it on purpose*, Raven reflected, *Kohlberg's "elected" officials doing their part.*

Each state in the union issued a call to their respective National Guard units for deployment to major cities; Congress debated giving the president emergency powers to use the regular military on US soil despite the Posse Comitatus Act. The president himself had reached a breaking point, with members of both parties appearing on television to suggest they had no confidence in his ability to lead and he should step down.

Their words sounded odd to Raven, more prepared and practiced than the usual rounds of talking head nonsense. It was as if the words had been memorized, the congressional reps speaking on command. More of Kohlberg's infiltrators? How many did he have installed? Would stopping the terror cells solve the problem, or would more Kohlberg sleepers remain hidden and continue to undermine the United States from within well after?

The scenario Kohlberg wanted was clearer now than ever. Get the military on the street, depose the sitting president, and replace him with a puppet. The US would then be under control with half the population falling in step with any new rules or "emergency powers". The other half would oppose such powers, yet the government wouldn't have to enforce them except in extreme cases. For the average American, their own friends and neighbors would argue the government's case, and shout down opposing views, trying to shame others into complying and reporting them to authorities if they didn't. Raven had seen it happen before. What Kohlberg and his "people" planned once they gained control, Raven had no way to guess.

It suddenly felt like Raven was in the middle of the toughest challenge of his life. With no end in sight.

He told himself:

Focus on the basics. What do you know?

Forget the big picture. You can't stop it. But you know the source.

Crush the head of the snake!

AS they worked through the day and Roger Justice used his computer to scan the late Carl Price's cell phone, many pieces began falling into place.

And Raven had to speak with Clark Wilson. Urgently.

41

"Are you ready for a data dump, Clark?"

"Mind if I record this?" the CIA man said.

"Be my guest and play it back till you get sick of it."

"Go."

"First, New York City. David Mark Graves. He runs a bar called the Horsehead. He hosted one of the Kohlberg cells. They hid in the basement.

"Second," Raven continued, "Carl Price is dead."

"We know. Him and a bunch of other guys."

"I wanted him alive but I had no choice but to kill him. The others you mention are part of the Horsehead cell."

"What else?"

"Couple names, from Price's phone, and you'll know them. They're CIA. Arthur Hunt and Emma Bell."

Wilson sighed.

"Clark?"

"Yeah, Sam. We know about Hunt. He's the one who caused your trouble in Germany. We didn't know about Bell. She works closely with him."

"Round them up. Between them and the bar owner, and

any testimony from the Weigels, and the tidbit I've saved for last, I'm sure you can begin dismantling the Kohlberg operation."

"What are you saving for last?" Clark said.

"Price called Kohlberg direct. Number stored on his phone."

"Are you—"

"No joke. Roger traced the line back to the vicinity of Kohlberg's estate. Can't be anybody else."

"This is a good start," Wilson said.

"For now, the goal is to stop these attacks. Get the president on TV to name Kohlberg and put pressure on him; might help. For as long as he lives, anyway."

"What are your plans?"

"We're going back to Germany. Kohlberg is dying anyway. You might as well tell the world why."

"Sam, be careful. It will take more than this to convince some people. If you murder Kohlberg outright, there may be consequences."

"I live with consequences every day, Clark. A few more won't hurt."

"Godspeed, Sam."

Raven hung up and tried to tell himself Clark didn't think he was on a one-way trip to the grave.

A grave with no name.

RAVEN FOUND Taylinn sitting on her balcony watching the skyline.

He closed the sliding glass door carefully. The sounds of the city weren't loud at the condo's height, but still present, unescapable.

He remained standing while he waited for a reaction from her. He expected her to tell him to go away.

She said instead: "I guess I can open the curtains now, right?"

"Taylinn—"

"You should have seen him, Sam. I didn't think—I mean, I *know* what he *did* and I *know* there was a side to Carl that was evil as can be, but, Sam, I never thought—he was going to *murder* me just *because!*"

Raven pulled another chair over and sat close to her. He took her right hand. He had expected her to tell him to leave, but instead she gripped his hand. Like she was grabbing onto a life raft.

He held her hand and remained quiet. There was nothing he could do or say to take away the shock.

"Is that why you—I mean, it's why you continue your—*whatever* you call it, right? People like Carl?"

"Yes," he said.

"There was no reason, Sam. And if it hadn't been for Lia—"

She stopped talking. When she let out a breath, Raven knew she was done talking for a long time.

EVENTS MOVED at high speed the following 72 hours.

Raven had a meeting with the Raiders and laid out the facts of life. They weren't going with him to Germany. He wanted them to stay and guard Philip and Leslie Weigel while they offered video testimony to the CIA over their part in the Kohlberg matter.

They argued, but they lost. Raven said he planned to take Erika and Rolf Ganser with him instead. His plan called for their specialties. And he didn't reveal what plan he had in mind.

CLARK WILSON and DDO Christopher Fisher pulled a team of internal security officers together and brought in Emma Bell and Arthur Hunt for questioning. They kept the pair in separate rooms. The security team began with an interview similar to any regular security review, but when the questions became specific, they knew the CIA had finally discovered their subversion. Hunt denied everything; Emma asked for immunity in exchange for naming names. Fisher was *very* interested in having a longer list than only the two of them.

WHEN RAVEN CAUGHT up with Erika in person, they embraced. It was good to see her again. He shook hands with Ganser, who was all smiles.

"Have trouble finding the place?" Erika said.

"Your clues were perfect," Raven told her.

Erika hadn't wanted to tell Raven their location over an open line, so she provided visual and geographical clues to a spot on the Florida Panhandle. She let Raven figure out the rest. With help from Roger Justice and his laptop, it had only taken a few hours to narrow down the location. Getting there took longer.

The Raiders exchanged their own greetings with Erika and Ganser, and then Erika brought them into a large sitting room where her parents waited. Philip and Leslie Weigel wore a few more worry lines on their faces since Raven last saw them, but they appeared in good spirits and eager to hear from Raven what the news wasn't reporting.

He explained the detention of Arthur Hunt and Emma Bell and Bell's offer to provide a list of names of those who belonged to The Fraternity. Weigel offered to confirm those names and fill in any gaps. Raven suggested he do so over video conference with the Agency; Weigel agreed. *That was easy*, Raven thought.

Raven next proposed leaving the Raiders for security while he brought Erika and Ganser to Germany. Weigel and his daughter hesitated. Raven told them he needed a chopper and a pilot. Ganser could fly if Erika secured the helicopter. Erika agreed on one condition. Raven didn't hesitate to agree.

HANNO SAID TO KOHLBERG: "We need to go. *Now*. Are you hearing me?"

Hanno scowled at his boss's back. He'd never seen the old man so slow to act. But it wasn't hard to figure out why.

The attacks in the United States hadn't come to an end, but the kill squads were meeting stiff resistance from National Guard units. He also couldn't reach Price any longer. *Nobody* Kohlberg managed to contact knew where Price might be found. After learning of the detention of Arthur Hunt and Emma Bell, he knew the worst-case scenario had played out. The operation to topple the US government had failed, and all because of one man named Sam Raven. The variable in an equation Kohlberg thought was bulletproof.

The old man stared out the window of his bedroom, hands clasped behind his back, chin thrust up. Like he wanted a sniper to shoot him through the glass and didn't understand why it wasn't happening.

"We have to leave," Hanno said again. He grabbed the two

suitcases Kohlberg had placed on the giant bed. "Now. Sir," he added.

"They can't win."

Kohlberg didn't turn from the window.

"They can kill me, but they can't win."

"If we don't get you out of here—"

"They can stop the attacks. They can round up a few of us. What they'll never cut out is the cancer I've injected, the people they won't find, who will continue my legacy. They will undermine that nation of vipers from Washington, DC, to the smallest of the major cities. We planted well, Hanno. The cancer will continue to grow and they can't stop it. A new generation will finish what I started. I only wish I could stay alive long enough to see it happen."

"You might, if we leave now," Hanno implored. "From the island, you can still direct and issue instructions. It may happen faster than you think."

Kohlberg laughed without humor. "Oh, Hanno, my old friend. I can never express what your loyalty means to me."

The old man turned and approached his head of security. "Give me those suitcases. I can carry them."

Hanno surrendered the baggage.

42

THE TWO MERCEDES SEDANS LEFT THE KOHLBERG ESTATE AT speed, running the length of the driveway faster than Kohlberg had ever allowed before. Both cars passed through the open gate and screeched their tires as they gained the pavement. Both cars made a sharp right turn.

Hanno told the crewmen remaining at the estate to keep the place tidy till the boss returned. Only he and the boss knew the truth behind the statement.

The security chief who had served Kohlberg for so long glanced out the back window to make sure their chase car followed. Inside the other car rode a four-man team of shooters with orders to escort Kohlberg to his private airstrip. Once the jet left the area, they were to return to the estate. Only he and Kohlberg would fly to the island, the location of which Kohlberg had never shared with any other member of The Fraternity. Once Kohlberg settled, the US and anybody else could search high and low throughout the world and they'd never find any trace of Oliver Kohlberg again.

Hanno watched his boss sit upright in the seat beside

him. The boss faced forward but looked withdrawn, possibly sad, though Hanno had never known his boss to exhibit such emotions in the past. The car ride was quiet and the road smooth. The driver kept the speedometer above the limit. They had to get to the airstrip where Kohlberg's Gulfstream waited as fast as possible. For all they knew, they had slipped away only minutes before Raven or some other form of authority showed up. Hanno swallowed. His throat felt dry and nervous tension filled his body. He'd feel much better when they were in the air and flying away from Germany, though Hanno hated to leave his homeland behind.

Kohlberg turned to him. The move startled Hanno. "Settle down, Hanno. We are almost there."

Hanno smiled and gave a simple nod in return. His mood improved. The boss was getting back to his old self.

Then they heard the helicopter.

Both men twisted around to see out the back.

Hanno noted an extension below the nose of the chopper. "Oh, no."

THE TWO-LANE ROAD wound through the forest. Raven grimaced at being back in such an environment, but at least they were far from any civilians. There was no danger to innocents. The only people who'd die were the ones who needed killing.

Raven cared little for the final destination of the two Mercedes sedans. Kohlberg rode in the front, the security crew covering the rear—standard fare.

He sat in the cabin of the chopper Erika had secured for the mission. Ganser flew the machine. "It's a big drone!" the German had remarked with a laugh. Erika had a viewing panel and control stick in front of her, too, but her controls operated the rotating-barrel cannon mounted under the nose. Erika's "friends" who supplied the chopper attached the cannon at her request.

"Have they seen us?" Raven asked.

"Tree cover is good so probably not," Ganser said. "Yet!" he added. "How close do you want to get?"

"Cut across the back of the rear car and blow them off the road."

"Copy."

Ganser drifted the chopper left toward the roadway and the gap in the forest the road created. The treetops whisked by beneath them like a plush green carpet.

"Brace for firing," Erika announced. She readied her controls. The LCD screen on her panel, connected to a camera on the cannon, showed her gunsight and the target.

The chopper cleared the trees and sped toward the chase car. Men with guns popped out of the windows—all but the driver. They opened fire. The winking flashes of their submachine guns forced Ganser to shift the chopper back to the right, over the trees.

Raven cursed. The cabin door beside him was locked. He'd wanted an open-cabin chopper; one had not been available. If he'd gotten what he asked for, he could return fire.

Ganser yelled, "I'm gonna sweep back fast; let 'em have it!"

"Go!" Erika shouted back.

The chopper pitched left, keeping pace with the two vehicles. Erika pressed the fire button on her control stick. The cannon rumbled and spit flame as the rotating barrels unleashed a stream of .50-cal projectiles. The rounds chewed chunks out of the road as the rain of lead crawled to the chase car. The bullets connected, shredding the roof and cutting through the center of the Mercedes. The chase case lurched right and flew off the roadway into the trees.

"One down!" Erika said.

"Good shooting," Raven told her.

The Mercedes containing Kohlberg increased speed, but the four-door tank had no ability to outrun the helicopter. Ganser laughed as he kept pace, Erika adjusting her sights for a second salvo.

Nobody fired from the Mercedes this time. Erika set the sights and pressed the trigger. The short burst destroyed the back right passenger tire, ripping through the fender, and turned the trunk into shredded scrap. Ganser pulled back, hovering over the road, as the Mercedes left the pavement and crashed same as the first.

Raven examined the crash. The front end was a crumpled V thanks to a thick tree, the ground sloping off the edge of the road so the car's front end was in the first while the raised rear stuck out over the road.

"Take her down," Raven said. He wasn't going to leave anything to chance. The Mercedes was a tough car. Kohlberg might survive.

Ganser lowered the chopper onto the roadway and kept the blades spinning as Raven and Erika exited with HK416s at the ready.

A man climbed halfway up the slope and raised a pistol. He was a younger man than Kohlberg. Raven and Erika split left and right as the man fired single shots, shifting his aim, not hitting either as he tried hard to hit both.

Raven came at him at an angle. The man swung his pistol in Raven's direction. Raven fired twice. One bullet plowed through the man's face; the other punched through his neck as he fell back from the impact of the first shot. Raven slid down the slope to the man and fired three more rapid shots into his chest to make sure this particular enemy stayed down forever.

Raven kicked forest debris aside as he crossed the overgrowth to the wrecked car. The airbags had deployed; the back was empty; only the dead driver occupied the front. He moved to the front where he spotted Erika coming down the slope to join him.

"No Kohlberg," Raven said.

"Look over there."

Raven turned where she indicated. A large lump of a man struggling to move on hands and knees and the groan he let out before finally collapsing indicated his condition.

"He'd better not be dead," Erika said.

They walked slowly, wary of a sudden strike, but they reached Kohlberg as he gasped to catch his breath.

"Forget your hiking boots?" Raven rolled the fat man onto his back. Kohlberg winced, shut and opened his eyes, and kept sucking down air.

Raven and Erika stood over him. The old man seemed unfazed by the rifle muzzles sneering at him.

Kohlberg finally found his wind well enough to talk. "You won't win," he said.

"You failed, old man," Raven told him. "We're rounding up your network as we speak, and your terror cells will be taken down within days."

Kohlberg shook his head. He chuckled. "So easy." He focused his eyes on Raven. "Do it. Shoot me. You'll see. You'll *all* see."

Raven lowered his rifle. "No," he said.

Kohlberg frowned.

"She gets to shoot you." Raven jerked a thumb at Erika.

Kohlberg shifted to examine Erika's face. His eyes widened in recognition. "Ah, yes. Tell your father—"

Erika's rifle cracked twice.

Kohlberg's last words died with him.

A LOOK AT: BULLET ALLEY: A SAM RAVEN THRILLER

BY BRIAN DRAKE

The past comes back to kill Sam Raven; this time, he may not survive.

An SOS from an old girlfriend brings Raven to Washington, DC, and soon he's looking for a killer. Jennifer Denosha married Raven's best friend instead of him, but now she says his old buddy is selling secrets to foreign spies. Before she can tell him more, she's cut down by an assassin's bullet.

It makes no sense—David Denosha is as big a patriot as Raven. As he begins to investigate, Sam discovers Jen wasn't lying. Her husband really is the bad guy this time. And Raven has to decide how to deal with him.

But David Denosha is not alone. A conspiracy in Paris is behind his wicked game, and the man in charge doesn't like trouble. He had no problem removing Denosha's wife; he won't have any problem removing anybody else, either.

AVAILABLE SEPTEMBER 2025

ABOUT THE AUTHOR

A twenty-five year veteran of radio and television broadcasting, Brian Drake has spent his career in San Francisco where he's filled writing, producing, and reporting duties with stations such as KPIX-TV, KCBS, KQED, among many others. Currently carrying out sports and traffic reporting duties for Bloomberg 960, Brian Drake spends time between reports and carefully guarded morning and evening hours cranking out action/adventure tales.

A love of reading when he was younger inspired him to create his own stories, and he sold his first short story, "The Desperate Minutes," to an obscure webzine when he was 25 (more years ago than he cares to remember, so don't ask).

Brian Drake lives in California with his wife and two cats, and when he's not writing he is usually blasting along the back roads in his Corvette with his wife telling him not to drive so fast, but the engine is so loud he usually can't hear her.

briandrakebooks.com